John Tudor, William Tudor

Deacon Tudor's Diary

John Tudor, William Tudor

Deacon Tudor's Diary

ISBN/EAN: 9783337007416

Printed in Europe, USA, Canada, Australia, Japan

Cover: Foto ©Raphael Reischuk / pixelio.de

More available books at **www.hansebooks.com**

DEACON TUDOR'S DIARY,

OR

"MEMORANDOMS
FROM 1709, &C.,
BY JOHN TUDOR,
TO 1775 & 1778, 1780 AND TO '93."

A RECORD OF MORE OR LESS IMPORTANT EVENTS

IN BOSTON, FROM 1732 TO 1793,

BY AN EYE WITNESS.

EDITED BY

WILLIAM TUDOR, A. B.

BOSTON:

PRESS OF WALLACE SPOONER.

1896.

EDITOR'S NOTE.

This copy of the memorandums of Deacon John Tudor it has been thought worth while to print, since many of the episodes mentioned by the old deacon were seen by him personally, and in many of the stirring events of the time either he, or his son were actively employed. The period of over 60 years, from 1732 to 1793, covered by the memorandums was the most eventful in the history of Boston and of the Commonwealth. The long contest with the redskins had ended in the previous century. The Colonists had already succeeded in their struggle for existence, and were very prosperous on the whole of the long coast line. The French held, however, the extreme Northern and Southern settlements, and had extended a girdle of strongholds from Quebec to New Orleans, and along the western fringe of the Colonial border from Maine to Georgia they with their savage allies were a constant menace to the outlying settlements of the English. The fall of Louisburg in 1745 was the first important success for the Colonists, but resulted in nothing, and it was not until the fall of Quebec and Montreal 15 years later that the French were finally reduced to their Louisiana possessions. The period from 1730 to 1760 was on the whole quiet and uneventful for the English Colonies. They had advanced rapidly in wealth and population during the first sixty years of the century. The immigration of the English had been rapid, commerce had taken great strides, and the coast towns had especially grown. While authorities differ widely as to the number of people in Boston at given periods there seems little doubt that at the end of the seventeenth century there were no more than 7,000 inhabitants. It appears probable that these had increased to nearly 25,000 in 1760 and that the town was then not only the most populous in the colonies, but with the exception of London was the largest and most prosperous English town. The Colonies had, up to this period, been left much to themselves, the English being occupied with their Continental wars and with the exception of a constant petty struggle between the Colonial legislators and the Royal Governors, no other interference with the liberty of the Colonies was attempted. With the coronation of George the third, however, in 1760, came a change. This man seems to have forgotten that he was king only by Act of Parliament, that the English were a people who had within less than a century beheaded one king and banished another, and that the American colonists were in all respects essentially English, with not only all the traditions of their ancestors, but for four or five generations had practically governed themselves. The subserviency of the English to the authority of the Crown had been gradually increasing ever since the overthrow of the Commonwealth. This was possibly due to the steady emigration of the prosperous middle class to America.* The king flattered no doubt by his adherents into the belief that the Colonists could be coerced into contributing to the expense of the many English wars, and knowing that he would be supported by a strong party in Parliament, decided upon a Colonial tax without the consent of the local legislatures. This act, which we must consider fortunate, since it resulted in the birth of a Nation from a union of the scattered Colonies, was not resisted by the

* The number of inhabitants of the English settlements of North America about 1776–7 has been estimated by different authorities at from one and a half to three millions.

whole people. The best estimates are that not over two-thirds, and in many of the Colonies not over half the people were in sympathy with resistance to the taxes. Amongst those who supported the Crown were the greater portion of the leading merchants and of course all the official class, which then was represented by, or connected with most of the wealthier men of the community. The closing of the Port of Boston, as the Crown's answer to the destruction of the tea, was an act of tyranny that could have no justification. The tea was destroyed by a mob, which had no official support. The leading merchants were probably entirely innocent, and they were the ones punished by the Boston Port Bill. No greater act of folly could have been done by the Crown, since it at once united all the disaffected Colonies, in showing them what each might expect if the taxes were opposed. It seems surprising after this that so few of the leading merchants were in sympathy with the patriot cause, as the commerce was nearly destroyed. The town's population fell off steadily from this time and only recovered slightly after the Evacuation by the British, as some months after there were reckoned but 10,000 people in the place. Nearly twelve hundred Tories went off in the British ships and the town can scarcely have contained more than four thousand people after the Evacuation, as Gen. Gage's census of the previous July gave but 6,573 persons outside of the military.

Up to the end of the war the residents had increased to twelve thousand, but not until the end of the Century had Boston recovered her former population and prosperity of the year 1760. No doubt the adherents of the Crown had carried away much of their wealth, and though many of them returned after the war, the town recovered very slowly.

The reader must picture to himself the small town

of Boston of 1730, containing ten to twelve thousand people; the peninsula almost an island at the spring tides and connected with the main land only by the then narrow neck across which Marlboro', now Washington Street meandered. All around the town were salt marshes; only a few winding and narrow streets; the great height of Beacon Hill and the connecting hills, towering above all the houses. There were even then many substantial buildings on King, now State Street. The houses nearly all had gardens and were scattered over a considerable area. Most of the houses were substantial though built of wood. The old town was probably much like Portsmouth, N. H., as it exists to-day, and resembled many of the English seaport towns of that period. The Castle, afterwards Fort Independence, and now Castle Island, was then far down the harbor. East Boston was Noddle's Island, and South Boston was Dorchester Heights.*

The following description of the old Deacon left by his grandson may be found interesting:

"Thus the old man continued his mem[s] until he was upwards of 85 years old and until he arrived at about one year and 5 months of his death. He died on the 18th of March, 1795, going willingly and wishingly out of this world. He was a man of strong mind and healthful body and remarkable for his integrity. His education was that of a common school. His personal appearance at the time that I can recollect him, when he was above 80 was very fine. Tall and erect, with long curling perfectly white hair and when walking with a broad hat and long cane, he was calculated to inspire all the reverence which can attach to an old man, who bears about him in his air and manner the evidence of a life well spent."

* See Lodge's Historic Towns, Drake's History of Boston, and Winsor's Memorial History of Boston.

The editor has added at the end of the book a list of the births, marriages and deaths of Deacon Tudor and his descendants to the 5th generation. This list is as accurate as it was possible to make it in the limited time given to the subject. The copies of portraits of the Deacon; his son Judge Tudor, and three of his grandsons have also been included, because these things are of interest to the family. The family coat of arms used in the book was furnished some years since by the English Herald's College, and appears to correspond exactly with an old seal recently found amongst the family papers. Regarding the origin of Deacon John Tudor, it is only known that he was brought to Boston in 1715, at about six years of age by his widowed mother, who afterwards married Capt. John Langdon. There was a sister of John Tudor's, named Elizabeth, who married Capt. George Mouat. From the date of her birth May 26th, 1716, it is possible that she was a half sister of John's, and a child by the mother's second marriage. At all events she died without issue Aug. 19, 1765. The mother is recorded as dying in 1763, at 84 years and must have been born in 1679, and was 36 years old when she came to Boston in 1715. The only further information about John Tudor's origin is the written statement left by him that his father's Christian name was William, and his grandfather's was Thomas. A short sketch of Col. William Tudor mentioned several times in the memorandums with letters addressed to him will also be found at end of the volume.

The editor is indebted to his brother Frederic for the use of the die with Tudor coat of arms and other family records; to Robert H. Gardiner, Esq., for copies of the portraits by Stuart, of Judge Tudor and his son William Tudor, the latter author of the "Life of James Otis," and many other publications, and to L. Vernon Briggs, Esq., for much advice and assistance in preparing the Diary for publication. This printed copy is as near as possible an exact reproduction of the original, the spelling and capitals being retained.

WILLIAM TUDOR.

BOSTON, October, 1895.

1732 June 15	I was married to Ms Jane Varney. We was Married by Dr Timy Cutler in Christ Church[1] in Boston at 9 O'Clock forenoon.
July 17	following went to House keeping.
Sepr 5	Was an Earth quake.
	This winter 1732 & 3 was Exceeding Cold Weather. The Vessels was frose up in the Harbor. 'Twas froze down to Long Island head. The people went Dayly to ye Castle on ye Ise.
The 15th of Feby	Was the Coldest Day the Old people ever knew.
1733 & 4	This Winter was as Moderat as ever I Remember.
1734	This Summer was Exceeding hot & Sickly. The people died in Numbers of the Fever and Bloodly Flox.[2]
1736 April 1st	I went into the Bakeing Business.
1737 April 26th	I went into my House that I bought of Mr John Burt Goldsmith.
1738 July 1st	The trucks run over my son Johns side of his Head and tore off part of his Scalp so that his Scul was bare 3 Inches.
May 1st	I left Docr Cuttlers Church & Joyn'd with Messs Welsted & Gray's Church[3] in ye Fall.

Admitted

[1] Christ Church was later called the Old North Church. It was the second Episcopal church built in Boston. It was from the tower of this church, which still stands on Salem Street near Copps Hill burying ground, that were hung the lanterns giving notice to the patriots in Charlestown of the intended march of the British troops to Lexington. Dr. Timothy Cutler, Rector, was born in Charlestown in 1683. Was made Rector of Yale College and embraced Episcopacy in 1722. Was ordained in England, made there a Doctor of Divinity and returned to Boston in 1724.

[2] Probably dysentery.

[3] This Church was called the New Brick Church. It fronts on Hanover Street, on the right side going towards the ferry. It was dedicated May 10, 1721, and originated from a secession of 24 members of the New North Church who objected to Rev. Mr. Thacher being called from the Weymouth church.

1738 July 16	Admitted regularly by Mr Welsteed to full Communion.
Sept^{r}	The Revd Mr Ellis Gray was Ordain'd Colegue with the Revd Mr Wm Welsted.
1738 & 9	This Winter was Extreem Cold & long. On y^{e}
5th April	at Night it frose Hard.
6th	Snowed Fast and Cold.
Decem^{r} 24	I was chose a Committee man, and so annualy many years.
1740 & 1	About ye Middle of April War was declar'd against Spain.
Septem^{r}	The famas Mr Geo. Whitefield came to Boston. Left us Octo^{r} 13 following.
1740 & 1 1740 & 1 Cold Winter	This Winter was the Coldest the Old People ever remember'd. Boston Harbour was Froes up twice. In Febu^{y} was the depest Snow we have had for 25 Years, There was a Tent kept on ye Ice between Boston & the Castle[1] for entertainement. Horses Cros'd Charlston & Winesimit[2] Ferrey Daily. Sledes Loded with Wood came from Charleston to Bartons point.[3] The
10th March	the Snow & Ice in some of ye Streets was 3 feet deep and lay in part til ye Middle of April. On the
5th of Ap^{l}	at Night frose very hard.
1743 June 17	The Battle fought by his Majesty King George the 2^{d} with the French at Dettingen in Germiany. The French army was commanded by Marshal Noialles. Prince Willm Duke of Comberland was with his Father in s^{d} Battle & was Shot in the Legg.
Octr 21	The total Eclipse of the Moon began about 9 in ye evening

1 Castle William, afterwards Fort Independence and now Castle Island.

2 Now Chelsea.

3 Barton's Point was at the extreme North End of Boston nearest Charlestown between what are now Leverett and Barton Streets.

1743 evening and ended past one Octo[r] 21[st.] Soon after the Eclipse came on a Terable Storm of Wind with Raine which continued all next Day, the Wind at N. E. The Tide was very high. The greatest damage has been done in Boston that ever was known in the Memory of Man. It would be endless to relate partickulars of y[e] damage To the Town of Boston; But the loss of Merchants in Sugar Salt Wharfes &c. is thought to Amount to a Hundred thousand pounds Old tenor.

1743 Dec[r] 13 The Rev[d] M[r] W[m] Cooper[1] died Æ[t] 50

1743/4 March The meeting house[2] at Roxbury was Burnt.

April 9th There was but 2 Ships in Boston Harbor.

1744/5 Febu[y] The large commet that has been Blazing allmost all this Winter has now appear'd in the Day at a Small distance from the Sun.

1744 June 2[d] War was proclaim'd in Boston against France. In England proclaim'd 29th March.. In France 15[th.]

June 3[d] between 10 & 11 O'Clock P. M. a Great Shock of an Earthquake was felt in Boston as it was on the Lord's Day, the people Run into the Streets from the Several Churches in great surprize.

Porto Bello Taken by Admeral Vernon 22[d] Nov[r] last by 6 Ships.

There was between 60 & 70 ships on both sides Ingaig'd. The Battle fought by Admiral Matthews in the Mediterranean lasted 3 Days, it began 20 Feb[y] 1743/4

From a London Print [of] July 5th 1744 [received] Yesterday

[1] Mr. Cooper was born in Boston in 1693. Graduated from Harvard College in 1712. Elected Associate Pastor to Brattle Street Church 1715. Ordained 1716.

[2] This church was built in 1741-2 to replace the old First Church torn down in 1741. The fire was supposed to have started from footwarmers.

1744 Yesterday, the Treasure taken by Admeral Anson Consisting of 298 Chests of Silver 18 Chests of Gold and 20 Barels of Gold Dust was Carried throw the City in 32 Waggons preceded by Drums Trumpets &c. with the English Colours & ye Spanish Ensigns under them. This Treasure was taken from ye Spaniards in the South Seas and lodged in ye Tower of London.

1744 Oct. 27 From the Jamaica Gazette. Satterday last ye 20th Instant happen'd as great & dredfull a Storm as ever was known in this part of the World, the Wind at ye begening was E. b N. and after much Rain &c.

Jama Hurekn It began about 6 in ye Evening & lasted till 3 in ye Morning, the wind was all this Time dve S. By this dredfull Hurricane som of the Forts was Destroy'd & many Houses blown down and all the Wharfs destroy'd. But ye Damage in the Harbour Exceeded that on Shore, for 8 of his Majesties Ships & 96 Merchant Vessels Wrecked & foundered so that out of 105 Vessels, only his Majesty's Ship Rippon rid it out withoute Masts.

Account of the taking of Cape Breton.

1745 17th June Cape Breton was taken under ye Command of Lieutenant General Pepperrell[1] by Land and Commodore Warren by sea; A city Exceeding Strong;[2] According to the French Accounts after the English had taken it, was found 9000 Shot & 600 Bombs, 148 ports in the Walls, 83 Cannon, 5 fine Brass Mortars & 1 Iron one.

July 9th G. Holmes & myself was chose Committemen of our Church.

Mr

1 William Pepperell was a prosperous merchant and a Chief Justice, as well as a colonel of militia. He was created a baronet after the capture of Louisburg.

2 The fortifications of Louisburg are said to have cost $5,000,000.

1747 April 10th — Mr George Holmes[1] & myself was chose Deacons of the Church where ye Revd Mr Wm Welsted[2] & Ellis Gray[3] are ye Pastors. Mr Holmes had all ye Votes but one and I had all but three. (Sd Holmes by reason of a pore state of health [declined] but beged of Mr Tudor to accept which he did in 6 weeks.)

1747/8 Jany 8th — I was Chosen Treasurer of the Society or Propriators of our Church — resin'd after 8 years.

1748 June 15th — This Day we have been Marred 16 years and by goodness of God to our Family & us, we have not had one Death in it til yesterday Died our negro man named Town about 35 Years old.

1749 April 7th — Set oute for Connecticut from Boston by Land and return'd in good health 22d blessed be God; I pasd through 25 Towns and arived at Norwalk where My busness was, which made 26. This Summer was the dryest our Old people ever knew. The grass and allmost everything was scorch'd up.

18th June — was so exceeding hot that people was in a Manner Melted at Meeting, it being Sabbath Day. When the Rains came on in August, the Seeds sown grew at an amazing rate.

1750 — This Spring & Summer has been as fine a groing Season as ever was known.

In March — The act pasd for Regulating the Gold & Silver Currency of this province.

Be

1 George Holmes was a Boston merchant and selectman of the town in 1750–52.

2 Mr. William Welsteed was born in Boston. Graduated at Harvard College in 1716. Was a Tutor there from 1820–8. Elected Pastor of the New Parish Church in 1728.

3 Mr. Ellis Gray was born in Boston. Graduated at Harvard College in 1734. Was elected Associate Pastor with Mr. Welsteed in 1738.

1750 Be it enacted &c. that it shall not be Lawful for any person &c., after the 31 March 1750 to receive, or pay any of the following Coin at a greater or higher Rate than is allow'd by this Act, followeth.

Lawful money Act — Vizt a Dollar 6s/ a Pistole 22s/ a guinea 28/ a moydore 36/ a 36/ ster pce 48/ a £3.12 Sterling, £4.16 An Engs Crown 6/8 an Engs half Crown 3/4 an Engs Shilling 1/4, an Engs Sixpence 0/8d, 18 Copper half pence 1s/, 3 Engs farthings 1d. Every person Receivg or paying Contrary to the above was to forfit 50 £.

1750/1 Feby 16 This Morning a fire broke oute aboute 6 O'Clock in ye Revd Mr Gray's Keeping Room, which Burnt most of Mr Gray's Cloths & most of ye Furniture in the Room but by a Number of frends his Loss was made up 10 fold.

1751 May 8 This Morning I was thrown oute of my Shay's by my hors's takeing a sudden flight. I was taken up for ded: I was most terably Bruis'd in most parts of my Body, so that I went with Cruches 2 months, but no Bone broke. Blessed be God for preserving goodness.

This May meeting I was Chosen one of the overseers of ye Poor for ye Town of Boston.

This Sumer & fall, everything plenty —

Decr 31 This night the Harbor frose up & remain'd so til the

1752 7th of Jany On ye

21st Jany I went from Boston on the Ice to the Castle with som Gentlemen & dined with Capt Larrabee* ye Commander. This Week many hundreds of people on foot and som in Slays pas'd on the Ice to the Castle & other places.

Capt

* John Larrabee was made Lieutenant of the Castle in September, 1722. He lived there, and remained in command for many years, and died Feb. 14, 1762.

1752 Jany 18 Capt Atkins[1] & I rode in a slay to the Castle, on our return we rode oute to the Channel whare a Number of Men was cutting ye Ice to open the Channel way for Vessels to go oute. The ice was 9 Inches thick, But they cut with Saws &c. from as low as ye Castle up to Clark's Wharfe[2] in 9 or ten Days & finish'd Jany 21st The next Day a Number of Vessells Sail'd.

March 24 This year 1752 the New Stile began & eleven Days was left oute between the 2^{d} & 14th of Septr and by an act of Parlement the Years begun ye 1st of January

Small Pox Year } This Morning Our 4 Oldest Children whas Inoculated by Doc^{r} J. Perkins[3] Viz^{t} John, James, Mary & Jane. 8 in Our Famely had the Destemp^{r} at this Time, 4 in the Natural way, all did well. Blessed be God for his Mercy to us & ouers. On the

23^{d} & 24th July the Selectmen and Overseers of ye poor attended by Several of ye princaple Inhabitants Uisited every Famaly in their respective Wards in the Town of Boston, and took an Exact Account of the Number of persons that have had the Small pox, either in the Natural way, or by Inoculation, since it first broke oute in Jany last: and it appear'd that 5059 Whites and 485 Blacks had it in ye Natural way, of whome died 452 Whites & 62 Blacks;

1970

1 This was probably Capt. Henry Atkins a selectman of the town in 1745–6, whose granddaughter Delia Jarvis was married by Col. Wm. Tudor in 1778.

2 Clark's Wharf was then the second largest wharf in Boston. It was located about where Lewis Wharf now is.

3 Dr. John Perkins is mentioned by Dr. Douglass in a letter to the Assessors of 23d April, 1747, as having a much larger practice than himself. He was still practicing in 1764.

1752 1970 Whites & 139 Blacks had it by Inoculation.[1] 24 Whites and 7 Blacks died. It is very remarcable how soon the Small pox went throw this great Town. It did not Spred in more than 20 odd Famaly's, till the begining of Apr[l] when those persons broke oute in Numbers who whare Inoculated the later end of March, and it went in general throw the Town. So that by y[e]

16 of Aug[st] folloing thare was not one person that had it. I was one of the overseers of the poor & My ward[2] this year was No. 3 I served 10 years N. B. In my Ward (No 3) Thare was Inoculated 120 Whites & 5 Blacks and not One died.

1753 Janu[y] 7 This Lords Day died much lamented the Rev[d] M[r] Ellis Gray aged 37 Years & 3 mo. He had been Ordained 14 years & 3 mo. He was Seized with an Apoplexy about 8 O'Clock A. M. & died at 2 P. M.

April 29 This Lords Day the Rev[d] M[r] W[m] Welsted died much lamented aged 58. He was seized with an apoplexy about 2 Minutes after he began prayer in the pulpit the last Lords day. The Congregation broke up in great Surprise and Sorrow. Thus Sudently was these two Godly Ministers taken from one church to our unspeakable loss but their gaine.

1754 Ap[l] 19 Last Night exceeding Cold. It frose 1 inch ½ thick. In y[e] afternoon Snowed very fast.

This

1 The method of inoculation for the small-pox was begun by Dr. Zabdiel Boylston in 1721, and was supported by Rev. Cotton Mather and most of the other ministers, but bitterly opposed by all the other doctors, led by Dr. William Douglass. Nearly all the people opposed the system, which, however, was finally accepted.

2 The town was divided into wards many years before this time. Ward 3 was then situated between the North End and the central part of the town, extending from the water as far west as Hanover Street, and including Fish Street where Deacon Tudor lived.

THE GREAT EARTHQUAKE.

1755 18th Novemr The Great Earthquake This great & Surprizing Earthquake in Boston was about 25 or 30 Minutes past 4 in the Morning. It came on like the Noise of Several Coaches rattling, there was 2 Shocks so Terable that t'was thougt if they had Continued 1 or 2 Minutes longer that Most of the Houses in town would have been shook down. The tops of many Chimneys was thrown down, Thousands of Bricks Slaites &c. Scatter'd in the Streets. The princaple damage was near the Town Dock. Many Thousands of people ran into the Streets in great Terror. Such Judgment may well make us cry out w'th the psalmist. My flesh Trembleth for fear of the & I am afraid of thy Judgments. 'Twas remarkable that not one person was hurt. Blessed be God for preserving us & our dwelings. Satterday evening folloing was another Shock between 6 & 9 O'Clock. Several small shocks was felt in many places for a month.

1755 Novr 1st was a great Earthquake in Lizbon. Numbers of Houses distroy'd. Many Thousands of people kile'd.

1758 July 26 Cape Britton was given up to the English. General Amhust commanded by Land and Admeral Boscowin by sea.

Decemr 16 to 20 I Mov'd my Famaly into the New house,[1] I Built the Summer past, on the Land purchas'd of Mr Edd Hutchinson last 30 March.

1759 Feby 2 This Morning about ¼ after 2 O'Clock we had an Earthquake, but throw mercy did no Damage

July 26 Niagara Fort Surrendred to Genl Johnson } French forts.

27 Genl Amherst took Ticonderoga. }

General

[1] This house was located on Fish Street next the water on what is now North Street, near Fleet Street.

THE GREAT FIRE.

1759 Septr 13 General Wolfe fought & beate the French armey Near Quebec. Genl Wolf & Genl Montcalm where both kil'd.

18 Oc^{t} Monsr DeKamsy surrender'd the Sitty of Quebec to ye English Troops ye 18th In^{t}.

Novr 14 A large Fire Consum'd a Number of Shops & dwelling Houses near Olivers Bridg^{r} Boston.

1760 March 20 This morning a Terable Fire broke oute about 2 O'Clock in the Morning at the Brazen-head E Side of Corn Hill.[2]

Great Fire Soon after the Fire got to a head the Wind Sprung up Fresh aboute N. W. which communicated the sparks to the S. E. part of the Town as far as Hunts Shipyard and about Fort-hill[3] and in 5 or 6 howers Consumed 349 Buildings. It is impossable to express the Distress of the unhappy Sufferers by the grevos Judgment. The loss to the Sufferers in Houses, Stores, Merchandizes, Furneture &c. was £100,000. Sterling. Colections was made in England[4] as well as in America on the acc^{t} I was one of the Overseers of the poor at this time & with the Selectmen Sat to examin the Acc^{ts} of the Sufferers & to distribute 1st to the Widows 2^{ly} to the Tradesmen 3^{dy} to the Midling people, the Rich had none of s^{d} Colection which came to about £55,000. Sterling there was many privat colections whereby many received in

[1] Oliver's Bridge was where Kilby Street now crosses Water Street.

[2] Corn Hill then extended as far south as Milk Street, where Washington Street now is.

[3] Fort Hill was entirely removed after the great fire of 1872. Nothing remains to mark its site but Fort Hill Square.

[4] Rev. George Whitefield was active in securing most of the English subscriptions.

1760	in boath ways full as much as they lost & some of the poore more, as fully appear'd; this affair before it was all Settled in about 18 mon[s] caus'd to the Selectmen & Overseers at least 100 Meetings, when the whole proceedings was laid before Governor Bernard & the Councle who apointed the Committee as aforesaid.
1760 August 2[d]	Governor Bernard came to Boston with his Commi[s] &c.
Sep[r] 8	Montreal Surrender'd to Gen. Amherst.
Oct[r] 25	King George y[e] II[d] died Suddently. King George y[e] III[d] was proclaim'd.
1761 Sep[r] 22	K. George III[d] was Marred to prenc[s] Charlotte. K. George 3[d] & Queen Charlotte was crown'd: they were marred som time before s[d] Crownation, and in general Approved of by the English Nation.

BIRTHS, DEATHS, ETC.

1760 Oct[r]	The number of Inhabitants computed at present to be contained in the known World at a Medium, taken from the Calculations of Riccioli & others, amounts to about 950 millions Viz[t]

	millions		millions
Spain & Portugal	10	Denmark, Sweden & Norway	6
France	20	Russia	18
Italy & adjacent Islands	8	Poland, Bohemia, Hungary & Tartary	50
Great Britain	9		74
Ireland	2	from other side	*79
Germany & Netherla[s] & Switzerland	30	Thus Europe contains	153
	*79	Asia	500
		Africa	150
		America	150
			953 millions

ACCOUNT

ACCOUNT OF BURIALS IN BOSTON.

1760	Buried Whites 508 Blacks 68, in all	576
	Baptized in the Several Churches	417
1761	Buried Whites 436 Blacks 81, in all	517
	Baptized in the Several Churches	374
1762	Buried Whites 390 Blacks 66, in all	456
	Baptized in the Several Churches	418
1763 uncommon	Buried Whites 344 Blacks 63	407 ; 11 more baptized than died
	Baptized in the Several Churches	418
1764	Buried Whites 471 Blacks 77 in all	548
	Baptized in the Several Churches	367
	Died more than Baptized	181
1765	Buried in Boston Whites 594 Blacks 51 in all	545
	Baptized in the Several Churches	435
1766	Buried Whites 389 Blacks 44, in all	433
	Baptized in the Several Churches	424
1768	Buried 369 Whites 48 Blacks, in all	417
	Baptized in the Several Churches	414
1769	Buried 579 Whites 66 Blacks, in all	645
	Baptized in the Several Churches	440
1770	Buried 404 Whites 79 Blacks, in all	483
	Baptized in the Several Churches	445
1771	Buried 423 Whites 59 (one newspaper says 63) Blacks, in all	482
	Baptized in the Several Churches	399
1772	Buried 458 Whites, Blacks 59 Bur[d] in all	517
	Baptized in the Several Churches	373

1773

1773	Buried 533 Whites 62 Blacks in all		585
	Baptized in the Several Churches		485
1774	Buried 546 Whites Blacks 50 in all	fleet & army in Boston this year	596
	Baptized in the Several Churches		521

1761 Aug. 12	We have had an Exceeding dry Summer. Scarce any Raine for 3 Months. Butter risen from 5 to 6–7 & 9s/ per pound Milk 1/4, the pasters burnt up. But this Morning Blessed be God we had a fine Raine.
Sep^r	Fine Raines.
Oct. 1 to 10th	Milk &c. begins to fall in price.
1762 Jan^y	Moderate Weather.
March 1st	4 nights & 3 days past Extreem cold.
17	Fine & warm.
War	Manifesto or Declaration of War published by the King of Spain on 16 Decem^r 1761 against Eng^d. The Warrant for a Declaration of War was given at St. James's 2^d Janu^y 1762 and War was declar'd against Spain the 4th
1762 Feby 12th	Martineco surrendred to the British Troops Commanded by Genl Monckton.
Ap^l 6	A cold & bad Snow Storm after a spell of fine warm Weather.
March 8	I was chose one of the Wardens of the Town of Boston. War was declar'd in Boston against Spain at 12 O'Clock on Wednesday 14th April 1762.
June 11	This morning about 11 O'Clock a Fire broke out in Boston in Williams's Court which consumed several Dwelings and Eleven Famaleys burnt oute; this is the 3^d large Fire besides the great one on March 20th 1760 that has happened in 3 years in this Metropolis.

An

1762 June 15 An Extreem dry season. But little rain for 6 Weeks.

Dry Summer } This Lords day morning about 3 O'Clock a Fire broke oute in the cabin of a Sloop that lay at my Wharf.

July 11th The Sloop was 1/3 burnt, the Cargo greatly damaged, and the top of the wharfe which was laid with Timber considerably burnt with a pile of Bords that was on the Wharf.

July 12 Continues very dry. The grass and almost everything

Dry Sumr scorched up, but little Rain for two months past

August Continues exceeding Dry. The dryest Summer our Oldest men ever remember. 2 dry summers going.

25 We recd the agreeable news of Morro Castle, on the

Havana Isleland of Cuba, being taken by Storm 28 July last

Taken after a Siege of 40 days. The English in Storming lost 50 men, the Spaniards 1500. 12 Augst the City surrendr'd

31 Yesterday and all last night fine Raines after a distressing dry Summer.

Sepr This month fine Raines & a growing season.

Oct. 15 This evening Pr Capt Hallowell in the province Ship we had the agreeable News of Newfoundlands being retaken from the French who had been in possession of it 3 or 4 months. It was happily accomplished on the 18 Septemr under the comand of Col. Amherst by land and Lord Colvill by sea.

Octr 23 Recd the News of the Prince's Birth Geo. 4th

Prince George ye 4th Born } Thursday Augt 12th 1762. This morning at half a hour past seven Queen Charlotte was delivered of a Prince. London St. James Gazette.

1762 Decr 25 A fine warm Day & fine Weather (except a Day or two) for five Weeks past.

Dec. 26th Very Cold. The Weather chang'd of a Sudden last night.

This

1763 Jan. 23 — This Lord's day morning extreem Cold. The Harbor frose over & continued so for 9 Days, when the 1st of Feby [came] the Weather Moderated & the High Tides together, broke up the Ice when several Vessells that lay below came up to Town.

Feby 2 — A Snow Storm at E. came on in the afternoon. We have had two large Snows in the 5 Weeks past and very Cold for the most part, but small Winds till this afternoon.

Augst — Plenty of Rain's all Spring & Summer. Everything plenty & Cheap except Meat & Butter, which is very dear.

Augst 10 — This day peace was proclaim'd in Boston with France & Spaine. Tomorrow is appointed for a Day of Thanksgiven for peace.

Decr — Most part of the Fall, till Christmas, moderat.

1764 Januy 10 — Extreem Cold 4 Days past.

12th — fare fine Moderat Weather.

23d — fine Day. Note: 12 days, fine Weather: no raine for 30 Days.

24 — A Snow Storm.

25 — fine Day, Snow this morning 12, or 14 Inches on a Level. Last night in a Severe Snow Storm about Midnight Harvard College was Burnt down.[1] The Large Library: The fine Instruments &c. &c. all destroyed. The General Court at this Time Sets at Cambridge on account of the small pox being in Boston.

Feb. 18 — This afternoon Mr Whitefield arrived in Boston from the Southward. Preach'd at Dr. Sewells[2] 2 A. M. to a large

[1] This was the college library then occupied by the General Court.

[2] Rev. Joseph Sewall made pastor of Old South Church in 1713. Died 1769.

1764 large and Crowded assembley.

Feb. 28 Extreem Cold this Day and Last night & 29th Night.

March 6 Extreem cold snow Storm, Wind N. E. a bright Stedy Northern light all last evening.

March 11 Extreem Cold last Night Very Cold this morning.

Friday 9 This fornoon our only Son Wm Tudor[1] was Inoculated (by Docr John Perkins) for the Small pox.

16 This Morning before daylight he began to complain of his head & back &c.

18 in the Morning Several of the pock appear'd.

23 & 24 Turned.

25 March Uery well.

25th A Cold N. E. Storm.

April 20 Last Night (being Thursday Night) we had a Severe Storm of Wind, Snow & Rain, at first Wind at N. E. which brote in the Tide higher than it's been for 40 Year: great damage was don to the Wharfes, Sugar, Salt &c. The Wind Shifted farther to the North before high water, or the damage mite have been much greater.

23 Very Cold for the season.

July 5 Last Evening we had here Terable Thunder & Lightning. It began about half after 7 O'Clock and lasted till half after 12. Blessed be God it did but little damage in Boston, but at Portsmouth it was more Terable and did som damage.

July 11 Extreem hot.

13th A fine Raine a fine groing Season so far: plenty of Fish, Mackeral are ketch'd at the wharfs, in many of the Docks scoons of small mackeral are ketch'd in such plenty, that they have been sold from 3 to 6 Coppers a Dusen.

We

[1] See sketch of his life at end of Diary.

FIRST STAMP ACT RIOTS.

1764 Sep[r] We have had plenty of Most of the Necessarys of Life.

Decem[r] 26 being Wednesday Last night came on a Terable Storm, Wind between N. E. & E. which Rais'd the Tide hier than it has been for 43 Years before, Much Damage done to Sugar, Salt &c. as the Tide over fload the Wharfes, fill'd many Cellars &c.

1765 Jan[y] 2 Extreem Cold day & Night as it's been for 4 Days.

9 Extreem Cold, but in the afternoon the Wind came to the South and it was much warmer.

Pork from 20[d] to 2/2 } 27 Extreem Cold.

30th Extreem Cold for 3 Days past.

31st Snow Storm; Every Nessacry very plenty. For 2 months past mostly Cold & sundry Snow which has made good sleding for 9 Weeks past.

Febuary Mostly fine Moderat Weather the Winter broke 11th Inst.

March 25 Yesterday (being 24 & Sabbath Day) We had a severe N. E. Storm of Snow the bigest Sea in the Harbor that our Oldest men ever see. The Tide the same height on a Level that it was 26th of Dec[r] last, but as the sea was so great it did Vastly more damage to the Wharfes & vessells &c. than in Dec[r] last. The whole damage was computed at least to ten thous[d] pounds Sterling.

Terrible Tide & Storm

Apr. 30 Pretty dry Season, for the most part of this Month.

May 1st A fine Steady Raine.

June 29 A fine groing season: provision very plenty.

August[t] 14 This morning was discouer[d] hanging on the great Trees[1] at the South end of Boston the Effiges of An[d] Oliver Esq[r] as Stamp Master & a Large Boot with the Divel coming

[1] Liberty trees. There were two of these trees that stood at the corner of what is now Washington and Essex Streets. They were cut down by the Tories in January, 1776.

1765 coming oute of the top &c. The Boot to represent Lord Bute &c. The effiges hung all Day and towards evening a number of people assembled, took down the effiges carred them throw the Town as far as the Townhouse,[1] then March'd down King Street,[2] and then proceeded to Oliver's dock,[3] pulled down a New Brick Building caled the Stamp Office, belonging to sd Oliver & carried the Wooden part of it up to Fort Hill and with Shouting made a Bonfire of it with sd Oliver's Fence which stood near sd Hill; and then surrounded Mr Olivers House, Broke his Windows & entred the House & destroyed great part of the Furniture &c. The next Day a Proclamation was Issued out by Governor Bernard and the Councel offering 100£ L. M. Reward for the discovery of any person concerned as aforesaid &c. Things remained something quiet till the 26th when toward evening a number of people assembled in King Street & Attack'd the House and office of Wm Story[4] Esqr Deputy Register of the Court of Admiralty (which stood near the Town House) Broke the Windows of the House and Office, destroy'd & burnt part of the Goods scattered & burnt most of the papers in a Bonfire they made in King Street near the House. Then proceeded to the House[5] of Benj. Hallowell[6] Esqr Comptroller of the

[1] The Townhouse is still standing at the head of State Street. It was built in 1714; partly destroyed by fire and rebuilt in 1749.

[2] King Street, now State Street.

[3] Oliver's Dock was located about where Long Wharf joins India Street.

[4] William Story went off with the British troops after the evacuation.

[5] Hallowell's house was on Hanover Street.

[6] Benjamin Hallowell was one of those proscribed as a Tory. His nephew, Robert Hollowell Gardiner married Emma Jane, Col. Tudor's eldest daughter.

1765 the Custom House; Broke down the Fence & Windows of his Dwelling house, & then entered the House, Broke the Wainscot and great part of the Furniture &c. and carried of 30£ Sterling in money &c. This brought it to the dusk of the evening, tho' it was a moonlight Night near the full Moon. Then the Monsters being enflam'd with Rum & Wine which they got in s[d] Hallowells Celler proceeded with Shouts to the Dwelling House[1] of the Hon[l] Thos. Hutchinson Esq[r] Lieu[t] Governor & enter'd in a Voyalant manner, broke the Wainscot, partitions, Glasses &c.; broke & distroy'd every Window, Broke, tore or carred off all the Famaly's Apparel Jewels, Books &c. and Carred off about 900£ Sterling in Cash, they worked hard from 8 O'Clock on the House, Fences &c. till about 12 or one O'Clock; when they got on the top of the House and cut down a large Cupola, or Lanthron which took up their Time till near Daylight, leaving the House a mear Shell. So great a piece of Cruilty (I believe) on so good, so inocent a Gentleman[2] was never committed since the Creation. The next Day the Governor & Councle Issued out a proclamation of 300£ Lawful m'y to anyone who shold discover the Leador, or Leadors of the Mob and 100£ reward for the discovery of any Actors in the affare. T'was supposed that several Contrey Fellows & saylors was concerned in this Mob, as there was but few of them known. There was a number of Boys from 14 to sixteen Years

1765 Aug[st] The Mob at Gov[r] Hutchinsons

1 Hutchinson's house was on Garden Court Street at the North End.

2 It appears to have been a general mistake of the period to suppose that Hutchinson was innocent of supporting the Stamp Act. See his secret letters to the English ministry sent over in 1773, by Franklin.

1765 Years of age, som mere Children which did a great deal of damage in breaking the Windows & distroying the Furniture Apparel &c. But what is surprising there was some hundreds of people looking on as spectators, I was one, that had they known each others minds they mite have prevented the Mischief don at the Livt Governor's; But there was such a Universal obhorance of the Stamp Act[1] which [had] past in England & was soon to be put in execution in America and which was the cause of the Mob's riseing and commiting such cruilty on the Governor; thinking he had som hand in the Stamp Act, but it was soon known that he was not only inocent, but had protested against it.

Aug. 26 The next Day there was a full town Meeting, when they Voted Vnanimously their utter detestation of the violent proceedings of the Mob &c. and had the minds of the people and the Inocence of Governor Hutchinson been known before, as it was at this meeting, the mischief at his house mite easily have been prevented, as the next day their was a Universal Lamentation for the Distruction don.

Augst 22 My son Willm Tudor entered collige pas'd examenation &c. and went to bording to the Revd Mr Appelton's:[2] Aged fifteen years 4 mons 11 Days.

Decr 13 Very high Tide. Provisions plenty, moderat Weather helther to, Butter 4/6 by the Firkin, Cider 30/ pork 20d,

[1] The first copy of the Stamp Act to go into effect the following November was received on the 26th May in Boston.

[2] Rev. Nathaniel Appleton born at Ipswich, Dec. 9, 1683; graduated at Harvard College 1712; ordained 1717; given degree of Doctor of Divinity 1771; died Feb. 9, 1784.

REPEAL OF THE FIRST STAMP ACT.

1766 20d, Hay 20/ old Tenor. Fine pleasant Weather for the most part till 31 this last Day of the Year, but now

1766 Jany 6 very Cold a large vapor on the Harbor and very Cold for 6 Days.

on the 2^{d} & 3^{d} Days fell a Snow 16 inches deep on a levell;

7th it came more moderat

Janu^{y} 5 being Sabbath Day & Small Tides & Extreem cold. Boston Harbor Frose over and on Monday it hardened so, that by Thursday people pas^{d} to & from the Castle on the Ice.

Friday the 10th it was moderat Weather.

Satterday 11th we had a remarkable Thaw & a South Wind, which broke up the Ice and clear'd the Harbor so that a number of vessells sail'd a Sabbath Day morning. This was very remarkable for the Harbor to frees up so strong & be so clear again in 6 Days. It was thro' owing to the s^{d} Thaw & high spring Tides.

Jany 10 We rec^{d} the melancholy News of the death of the Duke of Cumberland who died suddently at his House in London Thursday night Octo^{r} 31st 1765 in the 45 Year of his age; born april 15 1721.

March 12 We have had a moderat Winter & but little Snow, but

March 13 between 10 & 11 O'Clock came on a Severe Storm of Snow, Wind from N. to E. till aboute 10 or 11 clock on

Friday 14th when it Shifted to West & N. W. & blew Exceeding hard, by which several Chimneys were blown down but no persons hurt.

The 14th & 15th Extreem Cold for the time of Year; Snow 12 Inches deep on a Level.

May 16 This Day we Received the joyfull News by Capt Coffin[1] of

[1] Probably Hezekiah Coffin, who was Captain of one of the famous tea ships.

1776 of the Repeal of the Stamp Act,[1] which was signed by his Majesty on the 18th[2] of March last, upon which the Bells were Set a Ringing, the ship display'd their Colour, numbers of Guns were fired &c.

19 The Select men appointed this Day for the General Rejoicings and joy smiled in every Countenance. Our Goal[3] was freed of Debtors by the Generosity of som Gentleman. At 1 O'Clock the Castle and Battery & Train of Artillery fired a Royal Salute &c. &c. In the evening, the whole Town was beautifully illuminated: on the Common the Sons of Liberty[4] erected a Magnificent Pyramid illuminated with 280 Lamps. The 4 upper Stories were Ornamented with the Figures of their Majesties &c. To give A full discription of all the Fireworks &c. would be endless; all the affars was conducted with the utmost Deacency.

1 This was the first Stamp Act passed March 22, 1765.

2 The Repeal was reluctantly signed by the king on the 17th of March 1766.

3 This was probably the Bridewell situated at the Northwest corner of the Granary Burying Ground near the almshouse on what is now Park Street, or the old stone debtors' prison near the present City Hall.

4 The Sons of Liberty was a political society, mostly composed of artisans and young men, who were of great service to the patriot leaders at later period.

NOTE TO PAGE 23.

1 William Cooper was a brother of Rev. Samuel Cooper and a son of Rev. William Cooper mentioned above, and grandson of Capt. Thomas Cooper. He was born in Brookline Oct. 1, 1721; representative from Boston, 1755-56, 1774-75 and 1776-77; register of Probate for Suffolk County 1759-99; Boston Town Clerk 1761-1809, and for many years a Justice of the Peace He died 28 December, 1809. His son John married Elizabeth Savage, Deacon Tudor's granddaughter.

[BROADSIDE]

AT a Meeting of the Freeholders and other Inhabitants of the Town of Boston, legally qualified and warned, in Public Town-meeting, assembled at Faneuil-Hall on Monday the 21st Day of April Anno Domini, 1766.

VOTED, That the Selectmen be desir'd, when they shall have a certain Account of the Repeal of the Stamp-Act, to notify the Inhabitants of the Time they shall fix upon for the general Rejoicings and to publish the following Vote viz:

"Under the deepest Sense of Duty and Loyalty to our Most Gracious Sovereign King GEORGE, and in Respect and Gratitude to the Patriotic Ministry, Mr. PITT, and the glorious Majority of both Houses of Parliament, by whose Influence, under Divine Providence, against a most strenuous Opposition, a happy Repeal of the Stamp-Act so unconstitutional as well as grievous to His Majesty's good Subjects of AMERICA, is attained; whereby our incontestible Right of Internal Taxation remains to us inviolate:

"VOTED, That at the time the Selectmen shall appoint, every Inhabitant be desired to illuminate his Dwelling-House; and that it is the Sense of the Town, that the Houses of the Poor, as well as those where there are sick Persons, and all such Parts of Houses as are used for Stores, together with the Houses of those (if there are any) who from certain religious Scruples cannot conform to this Vote, ought to be protected from all injury; and that all Abuses and Disorders on the Evening of Rejoicing, by breaking Windows or otherwise, if any should happen, be prosecuted by the Town.

A true Copy Attest

William Cooper Town Clerk.

THE Selectmen having received certain Intelligence, that the Act repealing the Stamp Act, *has passed all the requisite Formalities, congratulate the Inhabitants of the Town on the joyful News, and appoint Monday next, the 19th Instant, for the Day of* General Rejoicing, *in Compliance with the foregoing Votes, recommending to all Persons a due and Punctual Observance of the Salutary Regulations enjoined therein.*

By Order of the Selectmen,

WILLIAM COOPER, Town-Clerk.

Boston, May 15. 1766.

Stories

From a London print April 18th 1766.
A Computation of the Number of Inhabitants in Each Colony and a proportion of Duties[1] which might be raised in each as an Equivalent in lieu of the Stamp Duties.

		Inhabitants	Proportion
Canada and its dependancies .		90,000	£3,000
Nova Scotia & its dependancies		15,000	500
New Hampshire . . .		60,000	2,500
Massachusetts Bay . . .		240,000	8,000
Connecticut		150,000	5,000
Rhode Island		45,000	1,500
New York		150,000	5,000
Jerseys		90,000	3,000
Pennsylvania Lower counties	210,000 15,000	225,000	7,000
Maryland		120,000	4,000
Virginia		180,000	6,000
North Carolina . . .		45,000	1,500
South Carolina . . .		105,000	3,500
Georgia, East & West Florida Bahama & Bermuda		30,000	1,000
Jamaica		150,000	5,000
Barbadoes		75,000	2,500
Antigua		45,000	1,500
St. Christopers, Nevis, Mont-serat, Granada, Dominica, Tobego, & St. Vincent		45,000	1,500
Total		1,860,000[2]	62,000

Divided by the total number of Inhabitants makes 8d each per Annum. It

[1] It was at this time proposed in England that the Colonies should vote

Monday June 16 1766 It has been hot & dry for aboute 10 Days past Satterday last, Butter & Hay began to rise, But blessed be God this afternoon came on a fine Raine sutch as has not been remembered in the Month of June, for it continued Rayney & Fogy til Satterday Night 5 Days & Night.

23 fare & warm and a fine prospect of plenty, tho' a backward spring till the latter end of May.

June 16 Yesterday (Sabbath day) aboute 7 O'Clock afternoon Dr Clarks'[1] Large Barn & Coach-house was consumed by fire. The Fire burst oute on a sudden and blaz'd with sutch Furce that 'twas a great Mercy that all the North part of the Town was not laid in Ashes, as the Houses was exceeding dry & the Wind Fresh & S. be W. The Sparks flew and catch'd a Number of Houses to Leward, but by the dexterety of the Inhabitants & a plenty of Water, under providence with the help of Indjains[2] we were preserv'd.

Decr 19 Every Nesaery of Life plenty, we have had fine Moderat Weather the Fall past, till this day came on a Snow Storm.

20 Snowed all Day yesterday & last night, so that this Morning Snow was 18 Inches deep on a Levell.

21 A fine day overhead.

Extreem

a voluntary contribution in place of the estimated revenues from the stamp duties, but the obstinacy of the king prevented this plan from being carried out.

NOTE TO PAGE 24.

[2] This estimate would give about a million and a half of people for the provinces that later revolted. John Adams at the beginning of the war estimated the population of Massachusetts at four hundred thousand. Burke in his appeal to Parliament for the repeal of the first Stamp Act speaks of the Colonies containing three millions of people.

[1] Probably Dr. John Clark, Speaker.

[2] Indjains—fire-engines.

1767 Januy 2d Extreem Cold for 3 Days past, Last Tuesday a Snow 10 Inches deep.

3d The Weather something more moderat.

Feby 4th Last Night just after 10 O'Clock Brays Bak-house in Mr Hancocks Buildings on the South Side of the Mill Creek[3] burst oute into flames, the Wind being fresh at West. The Flames & Sparks soon drove on the Roofs of the houses on both sides of the Creek & consumed above 20 Houses & near 50 Famalys where turn'd oute of Doars; A Number of Stores Shops and Barnes were allso Consumed. It was aboute 3 O'Clock in the Morning before the Flames were subdued, as it was low Water when it began. The Weather was so Cold that the Water which fell on Mens Clothes froze immediately.

March 14 Extreem Cold for 3 Days past.

July 17 Extreem Dry Weather all the Month of June past & till this Day when we had a fine Raine. Hay Sold from 35/ to 45/ ℔ hundred Roots of all sorts began to be exceeding dear &c. &c.

Augst 13 A fine groing season & plenty of Raine since the 17 of July.

November Provisions very plenty good mutton for 2 Coppers ℔ pound the best of Lamb for 3. Turkeys & Fowles for 2/ old Tenor, in short nothing dear but Hay.

1768 Feby This month quite Moderat, tho' the Winter Sett in the beginning of Decemr

Feby 20 But little Snow or Ice on the Ground.

March 15 Prity cold, but no Snow on the Ground, we have had but a tryfle of Snow for a Month past.

20 This morning (Sabbath Day) we had a Severe N. E. Snow

3 Mill Creek divided the North End from the rest of the Town and was located where Blackstone Street now is.

1768 March 20 Snow Storm. It blew Extreem hard last Night, it being just after the Change of the Moon we had a very high Tide.

Apl 1st A very Cold Snow Storm, Wind from N. to N. W. blew hard.

2 Extreem Cold last Night, blew a neare Harican at N. W. Which continu'd this Day & made as much Ice on the Bows & Sides of Vessells as in the Middle of Winter.

3d more Moderat.

May Raw Cold most of this Month; the Spring Backward.

June 30 The coldest Weather that ever I Remember for June, has been throw this Month; but we have had fine Raines and a prospect of every thing being plenty.

Septr We have had fine Showers most of the Summer past & a plinty of all sorts of provisions.

Septr 28 Recd Advice that Several Men of War and Transports was arrived at Nantsket.

29 The Fleet came to Anchor near Castle Willm.

30 At 3 O'Clock P. M. the Lanceston of 40 Guns, the Mermaid of 28, Glasgow of 20, Beven of 14, Senegal 14, Bonnetta 10, several armed schooners, which with the Romney of 50 Guns (which had been hear most of the Summer) & the other Ships of War before in the Harbour, Capt Smith in the Mermaid Comadore, all came up to town bringing with them the 14th Regiment Col. Dalrymple & 29th Regt Col. Care. So that now we See Boston Surrounded with aboute 14 Ships, or Vessells of war. The greatest perade perhaps ever seen in the Harbour of Boston.[1]

At

[1] This warlike demonstration was to carry out the second Stamp Act called the Townshend Revenue Bill passed in August, 1767, which provided that "The revenue was to be at the disposition of the king," thereby ignoring entirely the constitutional right of the people to vote their own taxes and making the king's power at once absolute.

1768 Octo^{r}. 1 Saturday — At aboute 1 O'clock Satterday all the Troops Landed under cover of the Cannon of the Ships of War; The Troops drew up in King Street and marched off in a Short time into the Common with Muskets charged, Bayonets fixed (perhaps Expecting to have met with resestance as the Soldiers afterwards told the inhabitants) their Colours flying, Drums beating & museck playing, In short they made a gallant appearance, makeing with the Train of Artillery aboute 800 Men. In the afternoon Tents was set up in the Common for the 29 Regiment and about SunSett the 14 Regem^{t} Marched from the Common down to Faneuil Hall.

Octr 1st — (having no Camp equipage arriv'd), where they stood about 2 howers, at last about 9 O'clock they were permitted to Enter s^{d} Hall: The Barracks provided by the Province at a great expense on the Castle remaining emty, which was the reason & caus'd so many disputes aboute Quartering the Troops in the Town

Octo^{r} 2 — Lords-day, the Town Quiet; This evening by order of Governor Bernard the Secretary Oliver opened the Townhouse & even the Representatives chamber for the Troops.

Octr 6th — Last evening the picture of Governor B^{d} hanging in College Hall[1] had a piece cut out of the Breast like a Heart & a Note left, giving the Reason.

Octr 15th — This afternoon General Gage arriv'd from New York just before sunset when the Troops where drawn up in the common to receive him & his Retennu, 17 discharges from the field cannon was fir'd to honour him, who

[1] College Hall was Massachusetts Hall near the west entrance to the University Yard.

1768 Octr 15th who came in his Chariot & 4, his Aid de camps on Horseback, all together with the Regiments made a gallant Show; Many disputes arose between the Governor Council, Justices & Selectmen aboute Quartering & Biliting the Troops. At last the General &c took up som Houses & Stores[1] at a great price to quarter them in —

1769 Janu^{y} We have had a great plenty this Fall, Fowls at 2/ P pound turkes from 2/3 to 2/6, Pork from 20^{d} to 2/ &c

Feby 17 All last month and the most of Decr was moderat till Feby com in & then it come on Extreme Cold So that Sled Loads of Wood &c past'd from Charleston to New Boston, and by the 12 of Febu^{y} the people pas'd in Numbers on the Ice over Charleston Ferry.

Febu^{y} 24 Uncommon fine warm Weather, 4 or 5 Days past, so that the Ice in the Docks went of faster than it made in the Extreme Cold Weather the 1st half of this month.

March 16 The Wind blew hard at South this afternoon; and about 8 O'clock in the Evening it shifted to W. & W. N. W. and blew a most Terable Gale all Night & the most part of the Day folloing. This Morning we heard of Deacon Lee's[2] Death: He Died last night pretty suddently Æ 90. The last of the Founders of our Church.[3]

Fine

[1] Mrs. Turrell says, "When the British Troops came here they were lodged in a sugar-house in Brattle Square."

[2] Thomas Lee was the seventh signer of the agreement of the 24 members of the New North Church that seceded and formed the New (Brick) Church of which he was made deacon and preceded Deacon Tudor as treasurer.

[3] The New Brick Church on Hanover Street, called the Cockerel Church on account of a weather-cock placed on the spire as a satire upon Rev. Peter Thacher, who was the cause of the rupture. The church was also

THE BOSTON MASSACRE.

1769 Septem[r] Fine Weather, a plentyfull Summer.

Novem[r] 28 Moderate Weather for the most part of the Fall, till last Night, when it came on very Cold as it 'tis this Morning

1770 Febu[y] 6 Extreme Cold Weather for more than three Weeks past except 2 or 3 Days, but the Harbor in the Chanil-way did not frees up the whole Time. There was numbers of people pasing from Boston to Charleston on the Ice with sleds &c; this Day a Gentleman from Lynn Rode over from Charleston to Boston in his shays, din'd with me & told me he Brought another person with him in the shays, and that it seem'd as safe Riding as on the Land.

8th An East Wind & som Raine the Ice breakeing up.

24 It Snow'd all Day very fast, About 10 O'Clock before noon it was very Dark & soon follow'd Thunder. At 11 it Lyhten'd & hard Roling Thunder emeditty follow'd. Very oncommon for the Time of the Year & Snowing so very fast at the same Time.

25 (Sabbath) Extreem Cold. The Harbor was skim'd over this morning with Ice; it was all clear the Day before, but the Ebb Tide carid it off

28 Extreem Cold for 3 Days & 3 Nights past, this Day fine weather & moderat

March On Monday Evening the 5th current, a few Minutes after 9 O'Clock a most horrid murder was committed in King Street before the Customhouse[1] Door by 8 or 9 Soldiers

known as the Revenge Church, and for a time this name was seriously considered by the founders.

[1] The Royal Custom House was on the corner of King (State) Street and Crooked Lane, now Change Avenue.

1770 March — Soldiers under the Command of Capt Thos Preston drawn of from the Main Guard on the South side of the Townhouse

March 5th — This unhappy affair began by Some Boys & young fellows throwing Snow Balls at the sentry placed at the Customhouse Door. On which 8 or 9 Solders Came to his assistance. Soon after a Number of people colected, when the Capt commanded the Soldiers to fire, which they did and 3 Men were Kil'd on the Spot & several Mortaly Wounded,[1] one of which died next morning. The Capt soon drew off his Soldiers up to the Main Guard, or the Consequencis mite have been terable, for on the Guns fiering the people were alarm'^d & set the Bells a Ringing as if for Fire, which drew Multitudes to the place of action. Lev^t Governor Hutchinson, who was commander in Chefe, was sent for & Came to the Council Chamber, were som of the Magistrates attended. The Governor desired the Multitude about 10 O'Clock to sepperat & go home peaceable & he would do all in his power that Justice shold be don &c. The 29 Rigiment being then under Arms on the south side of the Townhouse, but the people insisted that the Soldiers should be ordered to their Barracks 1st before they would sepperat, Which being don the people sepperated aboute 1 O'Clock. — Capt Preston was taken up by a warrent given to the high Sherif by Justice Dania[2] &

[1] Patrick Carr died not long after the public funeral. There were besides these five killed, six others badly wounded.

[2] Richard Dana was a Boston lawyer, graduated at Harvard College in 1718. Representative from Boston.

1770 March 5th & Tudor [1] and came under Examination about 2 O'clock & and we sent him to Goal [2] soon after 3, having Evidence sufficient, to committ him, on his ordering the soldiers to fire: So aboute 4 O'clock the Town became quiet. The next forenoon the 8 Soldiers that fired on the inhabitants was allso sent to Goal. Tuesday A. M. the inhabitants mett at Faneuil Hall & after som pertinant speches, chose a Committee of 15 Gentlemn to waite on the Levt. Governor in Council to request the immediate removeal of the Troops. The message was in these Words. That it is the unanimous opinion of this Meeting, that the inhabitants & soldiery can no longer live together in safety; that nothing can Ratonaly be expected to restore the peace of the Town & prevent Blood & Carnage, but the removal of the Troops: and that we most fervently pray his Honor that his power & influance may be exerted for their instant removal. His Honor's Reply was. Gentlmen I am extreemly sorry for the unhappy difference & especially of the last Evening & Signifieng that it was not in his power to remove the Troops &c &c.

March The Above Reply was not satisfactory to the Inhabitants, as but one Rigiment should be removed to the Castle Barracks. In the afternoon the Town Adjourned to Dr Sewill's Meetinghouse,[3] for Fanieul Hall was not

[1] John Tudor, besides being overseer of the poor for ten years, was a constable of the town 1738, fire-warden in 1752, warden in 1762, justice of the peace from 1763, and Surveyor of wheat 1764 to '73, and moderator at town meeting.

[2] This was probably the county jail, a stone building between the present City Hall and Old Court House.

[3] The Old South Church,

1770 March not larg enough to hold the people, their being at least 3,000, som supos'd near 4,000, when they chose a Committee to waite on the Lev[t]. Governor to let him & the Council Know that nothing less will satisfy the people, then a total & immediate removal of the Troops oute of the Town. — His Honor laid before the Council the Vote of the Town. The Council thereon expressed themselves to be unanimously of opinion that it was absolutely Necessary for his Majesty service, the good order of the Town &c that the Troops Should be immeditly removed oute of the Town. — His Honor communicated this advice of the Council to Col Dalrymple & desir'd he would order the Troops down to Castle William. After the Col. had seen the Vote of the Council He gave his Word & honor to the Town's Committe that both the Rigiments should be remov'd without delay. The Com[te] return'd to the Town Meeting & Mr Hancock, chairman of the Com[te] Read their Report as above, which was Received with a shoute & clap of hands, which made the Meetinghouse Ring: So the Meeting was dessolved and a great number of Gentlemen appear'd to Watch the Center of the Town & the prison,[1] which continued for 11 Nights and all was quiet again, as the Soldiers was all moved of to the Castle.

March 8 (Thursday) Agreeable to a general request of the Inhabitants, were follow'd to the Grave[2] (for they were all Buried in one) in succession the 4 Bodies of Mess[s] Sam[l] Gray Sam[l] Maverick James Caldwell & Crispus Attucks, the unhappy Victims who fell in the Bloody

[1] The prison on Queen Street.

[2] The four victims mentioned were buried in the Granary Burying-ground on Tremont Street.

1770 March 8 Bloody Massacre. On this sorrowfull Occasion most of the shops & stores in Town were shut, all the Bells were order'd to toll a solom peal in Boston, Charleston, Cambridge & Roxbery. The several Hearses forming a junction in King Street, the Theatre of that inhuman Tradgedy, proceeded from thence thro' the main street,[1] lengthened by an immence Concourse of people, So numerous as to be obliged to follow in Ranks of 4 & 6 abreast and brought up by a long Train of Carriages. The sorrow Visible in the Countenances, together with the peculiar solemnity, Surpass description, it was suppos'd that the Spectators & those that follow'd the corps amounted to 15000, som supposed 20,000. Note Capt Preston was tried for his Life on the affare of the above Octob^{r} 24 1770. The Trial lasted 5 Days, but the Jury brought him in not Guilty.[2]

March 20 Som part of this Month very Cold and we have had a long and cold Winter, but not so mutch Snow in or near Boston as in some Cold Winters past

July A Fine growing Time, Beginning of August prety Dry, but a fine time for makeing Hay

Septr Fine growing Time

Sepr 10 This afternoon the Town was surpriz'd by hearing that Castle William in Boston Harbor was deliver'd up by Thos. Hutchinson Esqr Leu^{t} Governor to the Kings Troops of the 14th Ridgement Commanded by Col. Dalrimple

[1] The main street was probably King and Queen Streets, now State and Court Streets, thence along Treamount (as then spelled) to the Granary.

John Adams and Daniel Webster both considered the Boston massacre the beginning of the Revolution.

[2] Two of the soldiers tried afterwards were convicted of manslaughter, and branded on the hand.

1770 Sep[r] 10 Dalrimple who had been from the 8 or 9 of March last Quarter'd at said Castle.[1] This Extreordenary step by the Kings order was the More Surprizing as no person heard of it till it was don

Sept[r] 30 (Sabbath-day morning) Aboute 6 O'Clock, died very suddently at Newbury[2] of an Asthmatic fit allmost universally lamented, that Excelent man of God the Rev[d]. Mr. George Whitefield[3] in the 56 year of his Age. He had been on a visit to Portsmouth, at which place and at Kittery & York he had preach'd every Day last Week, and was to have preach'd, the morning he died at Newbury, on his return to Boston, had not this sorrowfull event taken place His body was buried under Mr Parsons Meeting house at Newbury. Doc[r]. Eben Pemberton preached his Funeral Sermon at the Thursday Lecture Oct 11th, from 1st Peter 1st & 4th To an Inheritance Reserved for you in Heaven. The sermon was printed.

Satterday Octob[r] 20 In the morning it blew hard & increased to a terrible storm of Wind & Rain which brought in the Tide & Sea till about 1 O'Clock to a greater height than has been known for 50 Years (which I well remember was on the Sabbath day tho' I was then but aboute Eleven Years old) The wind in this Storm of the 20th was from N. E. to N. N. E. Great damage was sustained by the Loss of Sugars

[1] The editor can find no mention of this surrender in any of the histories. As Colonel Dalrymple held possession already, the transfer was only official.

[2] Newburyport.

[3] Mr. Whitefield had lost much of his influence before his death.

1770 Octob^{r} 20 Sugars Salt &c &c. Numbers of Cellars was full of Water. Wharfs overflow'd, many tore to peices &c. So that many thought the damage to this province alone was one hundred Thousand pounds Sterling, as they suffer'd greatly at Saylem, Marblehead, Plymouth &c. Aboute an hower or two after high Water the Wind veared to N. W. so that the night Tide was not so high by 3 feet, the next Day moderat

Novr 15 We have had fine Weather hetherto, no snow as yet, provisions plenty

20th We have now 8 Men of War in the Harbor of Boston; besides arm'd Schooners, under the command of Comodore Gambier in the Salsbery of 50 Guns

1771 Janu^{y}. 30 Fine moderat Weather perhaps as ever was Known. No snow all the Fall & Winter in, or near Boston except a little Sprinkling till this Day at noon, came on an Easterly Snow storm, but not Cold; plenty of allmost every nesacary, particularly Fish

31 Cleared up Moderat.

Febu^{y}. 5th came on Cold.

6th Cold Morning. The first vapor we have had on the Water this Winter, but no great.

14th Very Cold Yesterday. The Coldest Day we have had all Winter, and last Night was the Coldest we have had, for this morning the biggest part of the Harbor was skim'd over, but the Tide cared it off, this last quarter of the Moon it was very Windy uncomfortable Weather almost every Day. The moon chang'd this Day at one O'Clock.

20th Extreem Cold all this Day

22^{d} Morning Very Cold, but chang with the quartering of the Moon at 10 O'clock A. m.

2 days

1771 Febu^{y}. 24th 2 Days clear & pleasent.

March 14 blustring Weather most of this Month

Thursday March 14 This Day was published his Majesty's Commissions appointing the Hon. Thos. Hutchinson Esqr Governor in chief; and And^{w} Oliver Esqr. Lieu^{t}. Governor; The Hon. Thos Fluker[1] Esq$^{r's}$ Commision was Red last Monday appointing him Secretary.

April 18 Fast Day 8 or 9 Days past very Cold Westerly Winds 3 Nights, the first of this Week it frose hard, but this Day it grew warmer towards Noon.

May, June, & July Fine groing Weather.

Aug 4 Sab^{h} Exceeding hot toDay & for a week past.

Novem^{r} Provisions & everything plenty except Cider, which was sold Current at 4£ ℘ Barrel, Cider only. A vast quantity of English Goods imported this Summer & Fall as the non-Importation[2] was broke up first at New York that had been com into in all the provinces for near two Years past, on acc^{t}. of the Revenew Acts being laid on Tea Glass &c by the parlement at home.

Decem^{r}. 2, 3 4 & 5 very Cold

6th last Night came on a Cold N. E. Storm of snow which continu'd till 11 O'Clock this Day when the wind blew at N. W. & very Cold

Extreem

[1] Thomas Fluker was representative from Boston, 1756–60. Was one of those proscribed in 1778 and left with the British troops. He died in England in 1783. His daughter married Henry Knox, afterwards General Knox, in May, 1774, much against her father's will. Henry Knox was noted at the time of the massacre for cautioning Capt. Preston against firing on the citizens.

[2] The merchants and traders of Boston entered into an agreement in August, 1768, not to import goods from Great Britain after Jan. 1, 1770, and further agreed in October, 1769, that no goods should be sent from Boston until the revenue acts had been repealed, and so instructed the Colony's agent in England. See Meml. Hist. of Boston, III., p. 29.

Errata in line 1 of note 1, for "Fluker" read "Flucker."

1771 Decem^{r}. 24 Extreem Cold

27th More Moderate

31st 3 Days fine Weather. Provisions plenty. Six Men of War Winters in the Harbor

1772 Febu^{y} 11 & 12 Extreem Cold fine Sleding for 8 or 10 Days.

15 Very Cold.

17 very Cold in the morning, moderated P. m.

18 fine Day.

22^{d}. fine Day & warm S. W. Winds 4 Days past which clear'd the Harbor &c of all the Ice. The Winter which from the begining of Decem^{r} has been prety sevear sem'd to break up the 18 Inst and this

22^{d} it Thundred hard several Times, about 3 & 4 in the morning & uncommon Warm for the time ⌒ Year.

March 5 More Winter still, for this Day a terable N. E. Snow Storm.

6 Snow'd last Night, so that this Morning it was 18 Inches Deep on a level, and very Cold.

8th Sabbath fine Day

9th A Cold N. E. Snow Storm, A long Winter. Good Sleding great part of the Winter.

11th a N. E. Snow Storm

12th As much snow on the ground as there has been at one time this 20 year & this Day very Cold Wes^{ly} Wind.

13 More Snow

14th & 15th Westerly Winds, Extreem Cold in the Night and Mornings & Clear: a greate deal of Ice made in the night for several Nights and as fine Sleding as in the middle of Winter.

16th Extreem Cold last Night & this Morning a large Vapor on the Harbor 11 O'Clock gros Warmer, S. W. wind.

This

1772 March 16th This Morning died my old faithfull Servant, a Negro Man, that Lived with me about 34 Years. But the last 10 Years of his life he was Useless, more espesaly the last 7 Years. We supposed him to be between 90 & 100 Years Old. He Kept'd his bed, but one Day & Died very easey. It 'tis remarkable throw the goodness of God, tho' we have had a larg Famaly of Children & servants for near 40 Years til of late, and never had till this Morning, but one person that Died under my Roof: my Sons & other Relations Died abroad. Bessed be God for a helthy Famely & all other Merceys. 3£ coffin.[1]

March 19 A fine Day

20th a very Cold N. E. Snow Storm

21 This morning very Cold N. W. Wind. There fell yester Day 6 Inches of Snow in about 10 Howers, & we had a very high Tide, over all the Wharfes. So that we have had 5 Snow Storms from the 5th to the 20th of March.

24 & 25 Fine Weather, the snow goes of ver gradually

29 Cold N. E. Storm & Rain We have had very bad Weather all this month (2 or 3 Days excepted) as ever I remember.

April 2d A Cold N. E. Storm (Fast Day)

3d Snow'd all last Night & the Storm continu's exceeding bad, Snow's very fast 9 O'clock a. m, Snow 9 inches deep on a Level

Apl 24 Cold raw Weather all of this Month except 2 or 3 Days

May 2 Very hot for 5 Days past. This Day the Blossoms came oute fast, the Grass & everything in the Gardens grew

[1] This account of the death of the old servant was entered in another portion of the Diary.

1772 May 2	grew faster than ever I remember. Southerly Winds, most of the Time.
May 8th	Raw cold 4 Days.
25	Groing Time
June 22d	very raw uncommon Cold for 6 or 7 Days past. Wind from N. to N. E. & E. with small Rains & very uncomfertable.
July	Several hot Days and a drouth that shortned the crops of Hay, but at the later part of the month the Raines Came on, so that we have a pleaseing prospect
Augst 8	The beginning of this month fine Rains. On the Night of this Day at 11 & 12 O'Clock til about 1 we had the most Terable Thunder & Lightning that we have had for 20 years past, at one Time. The Levt Governor Oliver's House was struck with the Lightning, but little damage don to that, or any other House, or person. Blessed be God for preserving us & our dwellings, when the Heavens & the Town for near 2 howers seem'd to be in a Blaze, it rained very hard
Septemr 21	A great number of Young Children have died in Boston within a Month past of the Measles, but few grown persons died of it, in general (except the Measles) it has been a Healthy Summer
Septr 30.	The greatest part of this month has been vary Raw Cold, N. E. Winds, & a great deal of Raine, the Brooks and low Lands so full of Water that the like in Sepemr. I never remember
Octor.	A great deale of wett Weather
28	Yesterday a N. E. Wind & a high Tide. Last night a N. E. Storm, which continu'd till 10 or 11 O'Clock this Day and very high Tide. The wind vear'd to the North

1772 Octo^{r} 28 North a little before high Water & so to N. W. by 1 O'Clock.

Novr This month has been prity favorable. In the 1st of it Cider very plenty. A great deal sold for 30 / ℘ Barrell & allmost Every thing plenty, no Snow but a good deal of Raine.

Decr. 25 Christmas Day fine & moderat, no Snow till last Evening, which was not above an Inch & ½ deep. This Month so far has been very Moderat. A great favor, as Wood has been dear from £7.10 to 8£ all this Month.

1773 Janu^{y}. 13 This is the 1st Cold Day we have had this Winter

14th Snow fell about 4 or 5 Inches deep

15th Cold

16 Fine & Moderat

27 A fine Day & very fine Slaying 4 or 5 Days past

Jan 28 Snowed from 8 to about 12 A. M. & turned to Raine for aboute 2 Howers

Febu^{y}. 9. Good sleding for 3 Weeks. Last Tues^{y} 3^{d} was Extreem Cold. 8 Monday Wind at W. & N. W. blew hard & very Cold 9 Wind S. W. & more moderat.

Febu^{y} 21 (Sabbath Day) This Morning about 2 O'Clock a Fire broke out in Sumners Joiners Shop neare the bottom of Cole Lane,[1] as the Wind was fresh at W. it soon communicated to other Buildings & Burnt 3 Dwelling-Houses and several shops, the Flakes of Fire flew in abundance over the center of the Town, so that it was genarly thought the middle of the Town would in a few howers have been laid in Ashes, but by Divine goodness we where marvilasly preserv'd — on this Day in Servis

[1] Cole Lane, now the south portion of Portland Street.

1773 Febuʸ 21 Servis time we was again alarm'd by fire, but it was soon put oute, again at 5 p. m. this Day the Wind Sprung up aboute 7, & by 8 & 10 O'Clock it blew exceeding hard at W. & N. W. the whole Day & being extreem Cold & a dry Time our fears on accᵗ of Fire was very great.

Febʸ 22. Monday about 11 O'clock we was alarm'd again by Mr Ivers's[1] House (Neare the above Fire) took fire, but by the Activity of the Indine[2] men &c it was soon put oute.

23 For 3 Days & Nights Extreem Cold. The Vapor was on the Harbor all Sabbath Day and Monday it frose the Harbor over. On Monday Night it was suppos'd to be colder than we have had it for many Years

25 Moderated

28 Sabbath Day. Here is somthing Remarkable. Last Sabbath was extreem cold & blew very hard at W. & N. W., but this Sabbath the Weather was Soft & so Warm that it was like a Summers Day, small Wind aboute S. W.

Boston March 8 1773 This day was Town meeting at Faneuil Hall, when the choice of Town Officers came on, The Honorable John Hancock was chose Moderator &c. (I wrote the above by MoonLight in the 64ᵗʰ Year of My Age J. Tudor)

March 22 We have had much better Weather than we had last March til this day, we had a Terable N. E. Snow Storm all Day. This Day p. m. we where alarm'd by Fire. The New Courthouse by a Defect, or a small hole that was in the funel of the Chimney in the probate office [the fire]

[1] Perhaps James Ivers, warden of King's Chapel in 1782.

[2] Indine = Engine.

1773 March 22 — fire] got throw and burnt the Floor in the upper loft, som of the Winscut back of the Judges Seat &c. The Chimney was sett on Fire to cleane it, which set the parts in a blaze as aforesaid, but as spe'dy help was nigh it was soon put oute, but in half an Our it would have sett the whole roof in a blaze. The Books &c was all removed from the Offices &c.

June — We have had a fine groing Season, a great crop of Hay and a fine Time to get it in.

June 30 — Begins to be Dry Weather

July 8 — An extreem hot Day, A very dry Time, But one Shower for 14 Days. Butter riseing in the price. Aboute the midle & towards the later end of this month som fine Showers that renew'd the face of the Earth.

August — Prety dry.

Sept[r] — But little Raine

23 — Extreem hot Day for the season

27 — very dry Time, many Brooks & Wells dry, Calm Weather for many Days

28 — A fresh gale at S. & S. S. W. all Day and very warm

29 — Very hot last night & this morning, for the season till just before 11 O'clock the Wind shifted to N. W. & blew fresh, so to N. & N. E. which soon brought on a fine Raine.

Sep[r] 30 — Raine & so Cold, Wind about N., that there was a vapor in the Harbor & Docks as at somtimes in Janu[y]. owing to the are being colder than the Water; All

Octo[r] — fine Wether, a Day or 2 Exc[d]

Novem[r] — Fine Weather most of this month, provisions plenty

Dec[r] 4 — Fine warm Weather continu's

Fine

DESTRUCTION OF THE TEA.

1773 Dec[r] 19 Fine moderat Weather continued, till this morning som snow & cold & raw with frost.

Note. The Body of the people of Boston and numbers from the neighbouring Towns have lately mett at the Old South Meeting house (Faneuil Hall, not being so large as to contain the people) Supos'd to be from 5 to 6,000, and having Several meetings, conserning a Large quantity of Tea shipt'd from London by the East India Company Subject to a Duty payable in America. This

16th Decem[r] meeting was adjourned to the P. m. and after finding all methods failed, with those men to whom the Tea was consigned,[1] to send it back from whence it came, dissolved their meeting. But Behold what followed. A number of Resolute men[2] in less than 3, some say 2 hours time, Emtied Every Chest of Tea, on Board the 3 Ships Commanded by Captains Hall, Bruce & Coffin,[3] into the Sea, amounting to 342 Chests without the least damage to the Ships, or other property.[4] This Tea was worth 'tis said at least 25,000. £ sterling, as

[1] The consignees were Elisha and Thomas Hutchinson, brothers of the Governor, Richard Clark and Sons, Benjamin Faneuil, Jr., and Joshua Winslow.

[2] Only the names of a few of these, and not until long after, were ever known, even to the patriot leaders. This plan of dealing with the obnoxious tea was probably arranged long before, and the Indian disguise was a most effective concealment of their identity.

[3] Capt. James Hall commanded the "Dartmouth," that arrived first on November 28th, of which Francis Roach was the owner; and Capt. James Bruce commanded the "Eleanor," and Hezekiah Coffin the brig "Beaver," which arrived a few days later.

[4] The three ships were moored at Griffin's Wharf, now Liverpool Wharf, near the foot of Pearl Street. See "Gazette" of 6 December, 1773.

1773 16th Decem^r	as a great deal of it was green Tea. It was all distroyed, with as little noise as perhaps anything of the like nature was ever don in the Evening and all over & quiet by 8 O'Clock
Decr 25	Satterday. Moderat till 3 O'clock P. m. when the Wind sprung up S. E. & by 6. in the evening blew very hard with Raine, till 4 or 5 in the morning, when it Shifted to the South & blew exceeding hard till about 2, when it Shifted to West & blew so extreem hard that 'twas difecult for the women to go to meeting; and continued till sundown, when it began to abate.
1774 Janu^y. 10	Came on extreem cold which continued 3 Days, but as it was full Tides the Harbor was not frose up.
14th	More moderate. Fine sleding, provision plenty. The best of pork @ 2/
15	Last night Snow'd so, that by 9 O'clock this morning it was 14 Inches on a level, which with what was on the ground before made it aboute 20 Inches
18th	It has snow'd every day at times for a Week past
31	Still Cold, fine sleding for 200 miles to the Westward as Travelers tell us and Snow in general 3 feet deep. This Janu^y. for the most part has been very Cold.
Febu^y 1	fine moderat Day
12	Raine at Night turn'd to snow.
13	Snow'd & fell 8 Inches So that we have now 3 or 4 Snows laying on the ground.
14	In the morning extreem cold
15th	Ditto, fine sleding.
March 8	Fine Day. Prety good Weather this month so far.
18	Prety good Weather this month 11 O'clock A. m. Small Wind about N. Snows very fast.

This

1774 April 19 This Day moved from Boston to Cambridg with my famaly, Goods &c, into the House[1] that I bought of Mr James Bryant the 29 of last Novem^r

May 4 This afternoon it grew very Cold for the time ⁀ Year

5 Thursday morning at Sunrize Extreem Cold for the season. There was so great a horefrost last night as ever was Know at this time ⁀ Year. It was the opinion of many that the apples & other frute would be cut off by this frost. And so it turned oute. Almost all the apples was lost, cherry's & peaches (a very few excepted) was all cut off

June A fine season for Grass.

July A. fine crop of Hay. It sold for 15 / ℔ hundred & before July was out sold for 13/6

August 1st 60 Days have expired since Boston Harbor was shut up by that inhuman act of the British parlement called the Boston Port Bill.[2] Took place on June the first and which has been carred into Execution with all the Rigour, that the Fleet & army could exercise, by Governor Gage,[3] who was the General with 5 regiments & Admiral Graves with 5 or 6 Men-of-War & 4 commissioners.

[1] This house is still standing near the top and on the south-east side of Nonantum Hill, Brighton.

[2] The act closing the Port of Boston was signed by the King on the 31st March to go into effect June first following. The first news was received on the 10th May. On the 13th the town meeting passed a vote asking all the other colonies to join in severing all commercial intercourse with Great Britain.

[3] On the day of this meeting General Gage arrived in Boston and was well received. He ordered the General Court to meet in Salem after June first, where, on the 17th of June, the five delegates to the Continental Congress, to meet at Philadelphia on September first, were elected before the Court was dissolved by Gage's order.

1774 August 1st sioners. Most Consistently cruel has the British legislators acted in employing those fit Instruments of Tyranny to inforce the most inhumain Act that ever disgraced an English Senate, or distress'd a Loyal a vertuous & I will say (for I Know it) an innocent People (a few excepted) It would take up pages to describe the various hardships Boston now groans under. I therefore leave them to the honest Historian. of American Annals to tell the dismal story to posterity: and whil'st the Shameful Story rouses their Indignation of the treatment of their Ancestors, may it inspire them with Virtue & with Patriotism: May they animate each other by the recolection of what their Fathers suffer'd for Freedom, & never part with this noble boon of Heaven, but with Life. Note. Let it never be forgotten the Genouras & noble Colections & donations [1] that were rais'd and given by the Neibouring Governments & Towns [2] for the Releafe of the poor & distress'd inhabitants of Boston on the cruel Treetment as above

August 8 Extreem dry for 15 Days past, except 1 shower of ¾ hower

17 ditto, till near 5 P. M. when it Rain'd fast & continu'd all Night & till 6 nex morning. by 11 fine Day.— Blessed be God for this favor of Raine, for the corn & grass was in a Malencolcy way.

A

[1] A record of donations received has been preserved in the Boston town records.

[2] All the colonies sent contributions, from even as far south as Charleston, South Carolina.

[Newspaper Cutting.]

BOSTON IN NEW ENGLAND.

The following is a List of the Squadron in North America under Command of Adm. Graves :

SHIPS	COMMANDERS	GUNS	MEN
Preston	Vice Adm. Graves } Capt. J. Robinson }	50	300
Somerset	Edward L. Cras	68	520
Asia	George Vandeput	64	520
Boyne	Brod. Hartwell	64	520
Tartar	Edward Medows	28	160
Mercury	John MaCartney	24	130
Glasgow	William Maltby	24	130
Fowey	George Montagu	24	130
Lively	Thomas Bishop	20	130
Scarborough	A Barclay	20	130
Rose	Thomas Wallace	20	130
Tamar	Edw. Thornborough	16	100
Swan	James Ayscough	14	100
King-Fisher	James Montagu	14	100
Cruizer	Tyringham Howe	8	60
Savage	Hugh Bromadge	8	60
Gaspee	William Hunter	6	30
Schooner Diana	Thomas Graves	4	30
Magdalen	Lieut Collins	4	30
St. John	William Grant	4	30
Halifax	Joseph Nunn	4	30
Hope	George Dawson	4	30
Diligence	Jona Knight	4	30
Canceaux } arm'd Ship }	Lieut S. Mowatt	6	45
	Total	502	3,475

Donations received since four last rom Mr David Hoar, of Cambridge, 10 Poonds of sage and 10 Pounds of baum, dry'd from Pennsylvania, 150 barrels of Flour.

The above Adm. Ships with Genl Gages 12 ridgiments of Regs was fixed at Boston, to enforce arbretary Acts Parliament & tax the people without their consent, &c. [Comment by J. T.]

1774 August 18 A new face upon the Earth

Septr 2 friday. Very hot dry Weather several Days past, but at 5 P. m. came on hard Thunder & Lightning with a great Shower

Sep^{t}. 3^{d} It Rain'd plentifully all last Night.

5th Another fine raine most of the Day

Octr 1st Very dry & dusty

2^{d} A fine Raine last Night & this Morning

21 fine Weather for 3 Weeks, plenty of provisions.

27 fine warm Weather continues

28 fine Raine last night & warm Raine & foggy this morning

Novr 4 fine Weather stil

5 fine warm Raine

18 fine Weather this fall, but a dry season for near 2 months till Tuesday morning 15 when it Thunderd & Lightned hard before day 16th A plenty of Raine but this 18th in the morning a small snow & cold, but clear'd off by 10 moderat, but at 4 P. M. wind shifted to N. W. from the W. & by S. & blew hard and Cold & at 7 it snowed very fast but soon stop'd but it blew hard & Cold all night.

19 Blew fresh & cold all Day wind W. & in N. W.

21 Blow'd hard J. Stanly[1] lost in this storm

Decr. 4 Sabbath fine Day, uncommon warm

20 Clear & Cold

Snow

[1] Deacon Tudor's oldest grandson and son of Capt. Thomas Stanly and his wife Mary (Tudor) Stanly, the Deacon's oldest daughter. Young Stanly was at that time eighteen years old, and was on a brig commanded by Capt. Chas. Acworth bound to Boston from Newfoundland. The brig went ashore near Cape Ann, and one other man besides the Captain and young Stanly were drowned.

Errata in line 4 from bottom, for " four last rom " read " our last from ".

Errata in line 3 from bottom of text, for " J. Stanly " read " T. Stanly ".

1774 Decr. 22 Snow

23 Cold

28 Still cold and this morning came on a cold N. E. Snow Storm which continued all Day

29 Cold N. Wind. Snow'd last night so that 'tis 15 Inches deep

1775 Jany 10 fine sleding several Days

20 fine Day & moderat Weather all this month

Febuy 1 fine Day. All Januy very moderat weather

10 fine Weather & moderat, till this Day, when it blew fresh at Est & at 11 O'Clock began to Snow

20 21 & 22 fine Weather & uncomon Warm.

March 16 Fast day, which was apointed by the provincial Congress[1] which sat at Cambridg. No General Court has been call'd since it 'twas desolv'd last June by Governor Gage.[2] This Fast Day was not kept by the Church of England as it was not apointed by the Governor &c as

March 16 formerly. We have had fine warm Weather for 3 or 4 Weeks past till this Evening it Rain'd & snow'd but Warm for the season. The weather has been so fine and warm that in 3 or 4 days past the pasturs in many places is as green as at som times it has been the 1st April

17 Morning snows fast, by 9 O'clock 5 Inches deep on a level.

April 5 Uncomon dry weather, ever sence the 19 March, for the time

[1] The Governor had called the General Court to meet on the 5th October, 1774, but had changed his mind on the 28th September and dissolved it. On the 7th October, however, the delegates had organized themselves as the Provincial Congress.

[2] This was an error. There had been no meeting of the General Court since June 17 until called again by the Governor in the autumn.

1775 April 5 time of the Year, til this morning a N. E. storm of Snow, which fell very fast, that by 8 O'Clock A. m. it was 5 Inches deep 12 began to stop after it had snow'd fast from 10 to 11

12 A terable Storm of snow & Raine. Wind ab^t^ East & cold

19 fine Weather, but terable News from Lexinton, just after 6, this morning we had a rumer that the 1000, some said 1200[1] Regular solders, that marched oute of Boston privately last night had kil'd 30 men[2] of s^d^ Lexenton who where exercising: by 7 that there was but 6: by 9, but 3 & 3 wounded: that the regulars were gon to Concord &c &c. Rumor on Rumor: men & horses driveing post up & down the Roads; by 10 that the News got to Boston by 7. By 10 we heard of 2 or 3 ridgements marching from Boston under the command of lord Percy, with field peices, to get to the Asistance of those who where fiting with our people of Concord, Lexinton &c. By 11 we hear'd [that] Percy's troops[3] took Old Camb^g^ Road, that they where 1000 at least; people were in great perplexity, Women in distress for their

[1] The original force was 800 men, under command of Col. Francis Smith. This whole force would have been destroyed or captured had not Percy come to their assistance when they were entirely demoralized; and he could not have reached them in time had he not been given proper directions by a too truthful patriot; nor would he if the orders given to the town officers to destroy the bridge across the Charles river had been carried out.

[2] The actual loss of the Americans was 51 killed, 33 wounded, and 4 missing; total, 88.

[3] Percy's account in a private letter gives his losses as 66 killed, 172 wounded, and 23 missing; total, 261, including 18 officers.

1775 April 19 their husbands & frends who had march'd arm'd after them on the 1st & 2d rumor — By 3 & 4 P. m. the contry was all in Arms for many miles round [and it was rumored] that the regulars was on the retreet &c &c; by 5 that many where kil'd on boath sides &c. By 6 the firing was hear'd on the Hills & the smoke seen near my House [1] on sd Hills. By 7 they were drove by our gallent Cuntremen near to Charleston Neck, on Charleston, Hill the Genarl (Gage) had planted som canon on sd Hill to preserve his Troops in their retreet; here our people halted very prudently as sd Cannon mite have kil'd many & night coming on put an end to this terable days work.

20th All confution, Numbers of Carts &c carreing of Goods &c, as the rumer was that if the solders came oute again they would burn Kill & destroy all as they march'd, for they, when they began to retreet yesterday sett several Houses & Barns on Fire, distroy'd & stole a numer of Goods, Money, Plate &c &c.

22d Boston Shut up. No persons allow'd to come oute & our army at Roxbery Suffer'd none to go in, so that the people in Boston Suffer'd greatly for want of fresh provision, milk &c but by the 25, 26 &c people was permitted by a pass from Governor Gage to com oute,[2] but not

[1] From the top of Nonantum Hill, Brighton, close to the Deacon's house, there is a fine view of the valley of Charles river and the hills beyond Cambridge.

[2] General Gage had issued an order that on depositing their arms, any of the citizens might leave the town. A great number of arms of various kinds were deposited under this order; but Gage, having secured these, decided not to allow those suspected of patriot sympathies to leave, as he thought their presence might prevent bombardment.

1775 Ap[l] 22[d] not suffer'd to bring oute any provision, or Merchandise whatever. For as the report is the Admiral (Graves) claimes a Right, as plunder, to all merchandise &c, on a Supposition that the people are in Rebelion & should be treated as Rebels, as he and som others call 'Em. By the best account we have at present, the nomber of our people kill'd in the ingagement on the 19th was about 40 & those of the Kings Troops in Kill'd wounded & taken was at least 140, later accounts say 300.[1] But I forbare at present a farther Acc[t] & leave it to som faithfull Historian to tell the dismal story to posterity. On the 29th My Daughter Savage[2] with three of her Children took their flight from Boston to my House [in the] upper part [of] Camb[g] for saftey, two of my Daughter Thompson's[3] [Children] from Brookline was with us before, many others who can gett a pass are dayly leaving Boston, from those terable times, Good Lord deliver us.

[Passes]

1775 May 20 Permit Deacon Tudor & Lady & Mr Thompson to Pass the main Guard

(Roxbery) Jno. Hopkins Sec[y]

Cambridge

[1] See above. The British loss was 261. Snow (History of Boston) gives the loss as 273.

[2] Elizabeth (Tudor) Savage, the Deacon's youngest daughter, married to Habijah Savage.

[3] Jane (Tudor) Thompson, the Deacon's second daughter, married to William Thompson.

1775 Ap[l] 22[d] (Cambridge May 1775)
Permit John Tudor Esq to pass the Guards from Head Quarters and repass
1775 May J. Ward Secretary

(Such were the times that no person was admitt[ed] to pass unless he had such a permit)

May 12 My son W[m] took his flight, & broke from Boston by the roundabout way of Point Sherly[1]

13 My son Savage[2] got to my House with his Daughter Debby[3] and Pegy Coolidge[4] P. m. Satterday, by virtue of a pass, with a Wagon full of his housel Goods & some Bacon secreted, for no provision was in those Arbretary times alow'd [nor] by the Governor &c permitt'd to be brought oute, nor any merchandise or licuars of any kind, those (as is suppos'd) is design'd for a preay or booty for the Officers & Soldiers, Admeral &c of the Fleet, who call the Inhabitants of the town & Province Rebbels and say they shall be treeted as such.

17 This evening between 8 & 9 O'Clock a fire broke oute in

[1] This was probably just before the seizure of all the boats by General Gage.

[2] Habijah Savage, a Boston merchant, who after the death of his wife Elizabeth (Tudor) Savage, in 1788, became deranged, and never recovered, though he lived many years later.

[3] Deborah Savage was the fourth child, born 2d March, 1772.

[4] Margaret Cooledge was a widow, who resided with, and a friend of, Deacon Tudor's family for many years. See account of her death at end of April, 1780.

1775 May 17 in the Barracks of the 65th regiment on the south side of the Town Dock[1] in Boston occasioned by a sergant delivering oute Cartridges to the souldiers by Candle-light. a spark from the Candle set fire to s^{d} Cartridges. The building was soon in a blaze. Upon the discovery the Troops beat to arms, which being unusual on such occasions, caused great Consternation amongst the inhabitants. Som inhabitants repair'd to the Engine houses as usual, but to their surprize were told the Engines were not to be diliver'd withoute an order from the General. (he having a few Days before took them under his care). By this delay the fire got to so great a height as put it oute of the power of the people speedily to stop it. It raged till near 3 O'Clock next morning, in which time all the Barracks on the dock, with a number of Ware houses, about 30 in number were entirely consumed with merchandise to a great value; The merchandise was cheefly taken oute of the stores & put upon the Wharf, & mite have been saved, had not Admeral Graves in a tiranecal manner som time before taken every Boat from the Town, & at the time of the fire cruelly refused any Assistance. It was the opinion of the inhabitants that if the engines had been in their hands as formerly, or [if they] could have got them in season, the fire might have been stopped at the first barrack. — The Warehouses & merchandize consumed, 'tis thought amounts to 25,000. £ Sterling.

May 27 P. m. A number of the Massachusetts Forces with a party

[1] The Town Dock was an open basin of water near where Quincy Market now stands.

1775 May 27 party of the New-Hampshire forces, in all about 600 were attempting to bring off the stock upon Hog Island,[1] and about 30 or 40 upon Noddle's Island,[2] were doing the same about a 100 Regulars landed upon the last mention'd & fired on our men without hurting one of them, our men soon return'd the fire and the Regulars run off. But more coming from the Men-of-War our people put off & got safely back to Hog Island. The Regulars began to fire briskly by platoons upon our people, at the same time, an armed Schooner with a number of Barges from the Men-a-War, came up to Hog Island to prevent our people's getting off s[d] Island; w[ch] she could not effect: after this several Barges where towing her back as there was little Wind and flood [tide] against her, our people made a heavy fire of small Arms on the Barges and two 3 pounders Coming up to their assistance began to play on the schooner &c, & soon obliged the Barges to quit her (for she got aground on Winisimet ferry ways) and after the tide was partly gon off, our people set her on fire in the midst of the Barges crue, that kept a constant fire on our people to prevent it, after s[d] Schooner burnt to the Waters edg, our people got all her Guns &c. that was not destroyed by the fire, a great quantity of Cloaths[3] &c, 'tis said to the value of 300. £ Sterl[g]. This affare lasted all Satterday evening & Night & part of Sundy A. m., the stock was by our people all taken off Hog-Island, & som from

[1] Hog Island is now called Breeds Island.

[2] Noddle's Island, now East Boston.

[3] It is not quite apparent how these supplies could have been taken out after the burning of the vessel, though all the accounts of the time mention it thus. The schooner was probably stripped and then burned.

1775 May 27 from Nod^s Island;[1] to prevent them from being taken, or falling into the hands of the Army & Fleet.[2] — Perhaps history cannot furnish us with a more Miraculous interposition of divine providence. Although our Enemies kept a hot fire, both from their Cannon & small arms, yet we had not one Man killed & but three Wounded, neither of them mortal. the Rev^d Mr. Tacher,[3] minester of Malden, & judg Cushings[4] grandson, who where boath in the above engagement, gave me the above acc^t of the Battle. 'Tis suppos'd that there was at least 150 Soldiers & seamen kil'd by our people, our peoples heads was not only cover'd in the Day, but allso in the night of Battle. Salvation be ascribed to New England's God.

as

[1] Noddle's Island.

[2] This account of the skirmish follows the local accounts of the period, and was apparently derived from an on-looker. The small loss on the Provincial side shows the bad shooting of the British troops, and this was usually the case in later battles, where the loss of the British was always heavy as compared with the Americans. This skirmish and removal of the cattle was managed under the orders of General Putnam, who received great credit for the admirable outcome of the affair.

[3] Rev. Peter Thacher was born at Milton, 21 March, 1752; graduated at Harvard College in 1769; was elected minister at Malden in 1770; elected minister to Brattle-street Church, Boston, in January, 1785; was for fifteen years Chaplain to the General Court of Massachusetts; died at Savannah, Ga., 16 December, 1802. Was noted for his eloquence.

[4] This was John Cushing, the father of Justice William Cushing, who was one of the judges at the trial of those concerned in the Boston Massacre.

1775 June 17 Satterday, as terable a Day as ever I saw, for Yesterday Genl Putnam[1] (a gallant man from Connec^t) was intrenching on Bunkers Hill[2] at Charleston, when a number of Men-of-War haled up near s^d Town to cover the landing of the regular Troops, about 3,000. with doble officers to command them against Putnams men, about 800. when [news of] the affair got to Cambridge where the Americans were incampt'd Gen: Ward[3] sent 1,000. Men to assist our brave Men, but they came to late,[4] for the regulars had got posesion of the Hill, 'tho' our people fought like herows & kil'd princaple officers 92 — Sargents 102, Corporals 100 & privats 753 in all 1047, besides a great number wounded many of whome died,[5] So that they got the Hill at a terable dear rate 1047 killed 445 wounded, 1492 killed & wounded: our people lost but 108 killed, 292 wounded, in all 400.[6] The

[1] This appears an error. Putnam was a subordinate in this battle Colonel Prescott having chief command, though Putnam had charge of building the breastworks on Bunker Hill, where he tried in vain to make a last stand.

[2] Named after George Bunker, the greatest land-owner in Charlestown, who died in 1664. The error in naming the battle after Bunker Hill is not quite clear, except that being the highest hill it was naturally supposed that it had been chosen for defence. The whole battle was confined to Breed's Hill, which Gridley the engineer planned for defence.

[3] Gen. Artemas Ward was then in command of all the Provincial forces near Boston.

[4] The reinforcements did not come too late, but they did not succeed in crossing the Charlestown neck on account of the British fleet and batteries, which swept this place, though the retreating Provincials do not appear to have suffered greatly in crossing.

[5] The actual loss of the British was 1,054 killed and wounded, including 157 officers, many of whom were shot by their own men.

[6] The Americans lost 420 killed and wounded, and 30 prisoners.

1775 June 17 Satterday, The Regul's lost near 10 to 1. about 2 O'Clock on s^d day the Men-of-War & there Boats-crew began to sett the Town of Charleston on fire,[1] and by 5 I saw the whole Town in flames: it contain'd 300 dweling Houses, besides Stores, shops &c

July 13 My son W^m was this Day[2] at Cambridge apointed Judg Advocate to the Continental Army, which we hear Consists of 35 Rigiments[3]

19 The Representetives mett at Watertown for the Election of Counciler's, & a Sermon was preach'd by Mr Gordin[4] from

20 This day was Kept'd as a Day of Prayer, & Fasting throw the Contenent on account of the times. 'tis said this is the 1st time the Collonys ever united to Keep such a Day at the same time. — It was agreed on last Month by the Contenential Congress setting at Philadelp'a

Lection-day

[1] The town was fired by red-hot shot from Copp's Hill in Boston, where the British had a battery. Little credit appears to have been given the British soldiers for courage in this battle, even their officers accusing them of cowardice. Considering, however, the terrible fire of the Americans, by which one company of the Fifty-second Regiment was wholly destroyed, and that of the British troops nearly half of those engaged were killed or wounded, and that some of them charged more than three times, one can but conclude that they were as courageous as men can ever be.

[2] This was ten days after General Washington had taken command of the troops at Cambridge. The appointment was not confirmed until July 29.

[3] Contemporary accounts give the number of Provincial troops at this time under the command of General Ward as 14,000, of which 9,000 were Massachusetts men.

[4] Rev. William Gordon was born at Hitchin, Hertfordshire, England, in 1730; came to America in 1770; received honorary degree of A. M. at Harvard College in 1772, and at Yale College in 1773; ordained minister of the Third Church, Roxbury, in 1772, and made Chaplain to Provincial Congress of Massachusetts. Returned to England in 1786, and published a history of the United States there in 1788. Died at Ipswich, October, 1807.

THE AMERICANS BOMBARD THE TOWN.

1775 July 19	Lection-day, there was 209 Representatives return'd to sett in the Court; They chose 28 counsellors. By the Newspaper, Watertown July 24th there was an account of 266 towns & districts in the Province ⌒ Massacts. Bay, many small Towns sent no Represnts. many sent too
August 1	We have had a very dry Summer, except a few Showers Hay fell short, but a plenty of all kinds of frute & a good Crop of Indian Corn in Octor.
Novemr 11	A great deale of Rain within 6 Weeks, but no Snow and but little Cold Weather
Decr. 24	For 3 days past very Cold, & this morning Came on a cold N. E. Storm & snow
1776 Feb 29	Very cold
March 1	Extreem Cold for the time o ⌒ Year, we have had but little Snow this Winter at or near Cambridge and none above 3, or 4 Inches deep as yet
March 2d	Satterday night about 11 O'Clock the Bum Batterys from Prospect Hill[1] & Leachmor's Point[2] began to fire their bums & shot against Boston, & Bunkers hill (which was boath ocupied by the Regulars) which continued on boath sides the best part of the Night.
Sundy the 3d	We hear'd fireing Several times, and in the Evening went at it again
The 4th	Aboute 7 O'Clock our people began from all parts to fire most terably at Boston (as afterwards we hear'd) to draw the Enemis attention towards our firing, while our people

[1] In Somerville, about one and a half miles west of Bunker Hill. This hill, and Winter Hill one mile further west, had been fortified by General Putnam before Washington's arrival at Cambridge.

[2] Leachmere's Point was between the two lower Cambridge bridges, nearest the East Cambridge bridge on the west side of Charles River.

1776 March 4th people to a great number of men & Teams &c took possession of two Hills[1] at Dorchester, Aboute 7 P. m. just as night came on & began to erect a strong brest-work, or forts, which they compleated before Sunrise. when the Generals, Admiral &c discover'd [this] in the morning they were Struck with surprize (& as we hear'd said the Divel must help the Yankey's as they call us.)

5th aboute 10 A. m. they began to fire from Boston, the blockhouse[2] on the Neck[3] &c, which was return'd by our people at Roxbery &c

6 Last night a terable storm of wind aboute South & no fireing, but the wind rored like Cannon

7th fast Day. Fireing seas'd on boath Sides

8 Still quiet, but hear the women & children are moveing with their efects on board the Ships, & all in confuton in Boston.

9th Quiet all day, but about ½ after 8 P. m. a fireing began from Boston, & continued all night on boath sides. On dorchester side 800 Shot was gathered up next day perhaps not half that was fired at them

10 All seems quiet 11 d° 12 d°.

13 Som fireing last night

14 Quiet last night & this day 15 & 16 do.

17th We were agreeably surpriz'd at the account of the Regulars

[1] The chief fortification was on the highest hill, near the centre of the Neck, though it was intended to strongly fortify Nook's Hill, nearer Boston, had the British remained. Only a small breastwork was erected there, on March 17.

[2] The old fort at the entrance on the south side of Boston.

[3] The road leading across the narrow neck connecting Boston with Roxbury was then called Orange Street.

1776 March 17th Regulars all leaveing Boston by 10 O'Clock this forenoon[1] (Sabbath) & that the Men-of-War & transports full of Soldiers was going of, & no fireing on either side: Bunker's hill was allso evacuated & all this without Bloodshed, was truly Surpriseing. The accounts aded also that the Selectmen[2] of Boston was com to Roxbery to acquaint and consult with our Generals on affairs.
And the Town of Boston was soon Enter'd by the troops of the 13 United Colonies of North America commanded by the brave General Washington, numbers of our people soon went into the Town and report that the Regulars went off in such confution, that they left near a 100 horses &c, sever'l Cannon & a great number Shot: with the fleet went of the Mandamas Counclrs[3] & a number of the other Tory's & famaly's.[4]

18 The Men of War lay below & near the Castle —

19th Easterly winds, they lay as Yesterday

20th this morning before Sunrise som ship or Ships of War drew up near the lower point of Dorchester were our people was throwing up a new brestwork to anoy the Castle, Sd Men of War fired near two houers at them but did no damage

last

[1] The evacuation had been long contemplated, but was carried out with some precipitation after the erection of the battery on Nook's Hill, Dorchester, which commanded the town.

[2] These were John Scollay, Timothy Newell, Samuel Austin, Oliver Wendell, and John Pitts. John Hancock and Thomas Marshall were also nominally Selectmen during the siege, but were elsewhere.

[3] These were the councillors appointed by the Governor after the charter had been set aside.

[4] The list of these given in "Memorial History of Boston," with their families, amounted to 927 persons. See Mass. H. Soc. P., December, 1880, p. 266.

1776 March 21 last night the Regulars burnt & destroy'd the Castle & left it [in the] P. m. our people took possession of it.

22d & 23 The men of War & Transports had fallen down from their laying near the Castle to Nantasket Road & there lay Several Days Windbound,

About 27 & 28 The Men a War & Transports & a number of Tory's with their Famalys Sail'd, & we after som days hear'd they got to Hallefax in a miserable condition, for want of room's and allmost all other nessacarys of Life, as they fled in hast

May 17 (Fryday) A Contenential Fast was Kept in 13 Provences — This Day was taken by one of our priveteers a ship of 300 Tons with 1,500 Barrils of powder, a 1000 Stand of Armes &c. &c, coming to Boston for the use of the Kings Troops, but luckely fell into our hands

29 Lection Day, We had the melancoly news that was rumer'd 8 or 10 Days before, confermed, of our people raiseing the siege against Quebec,[1] leaving their Cannon, baggage &c behind them. Some Men of War & Troops being just Arived to releave the garison & who with the old Troops came oute & put our Troops off. The General Court met at the meeting hous in Watertown (as the smallpox was in Boston). The Honorable James Warren[2] Esqr. was unanimously Chosen Speaker &

[1] Montreal had been captured by the expedition of Benedict Arnold and Montgomery, but the latter was killed in the first attack on Quebec, and the siege had to be abandoned, though Arnold succeeded in bringing off what remained of his men and munitions.

[2] James Warren, a merchant of Plymouth, was born there 28 September, 1726; graduated at Harvard College in 1745; was a member of the General Court of Massachusetts from 1766–74; died 27 November,

1776 May 29 & Sam[l]. Freeman [1] Esq[r] Clerk. The number returned to represent the Towns & Districts was 267, about 14 return'd afterwards, the largest number perhaps ever known in the Colony. The Town of Boston sent 12 Roxbury 3 Salem 6 Cambridge 4. Several Towns as well as Boston sent 3 times the number that they formerly did on acc[t]. of the Times.

28 Counsellors chose, 6 who were in last Year resign'd previous to the Election

June 13 This evening a number of men from Boston & other Towns embarked for Long Island, Nantasket Hill &c, where in a few hours they threw up a Line of Defence & planted som Cannon, & soon fired at the Commodore a 50 Gun Ship; upon which a Signal was made for the whole fleet, consisting of 8 ships 2 Snows, 2 Brigs & 1 Schooner to remove, & got of as fast as posable from Nantasket road where they all lay. The Commodore stopt'd near the Light House & blew it up; in the above Ingagement (for the Commodore return'd the Shot) not one of our Men were hurt. 6 or 7 Of the above Ships were full of Soldiers bound into Boston, expecting to join General How & Company not hearing of their being gon.

In Congress. July 4 — 1776 A Declaration of the United States of America in General Congress assembled (viz[t] 13 Provinces).

When

1808. His wife, Mercy Otis, was a sister of James Otis, and a brilliant writer.

[1] Samuel Freeman was born in Maine 15 June, 1743; a member of the Provincial Congress of Massachusetts for four years; was from 1775 for forty-five years Clerk of the Courts; was Judge from 1804 to 1820; died at Portland, Me., 2 September, 1831.

1776 In Congress. When in the course of human events it becomes neces-
July 4—1776 sary for one people to dissolve the political bands which have connected them with another &c &c

(The Congress say) The history of the present King of Great Britain is a history of repeated injuries &c all having in direct object the establishing of an absolute tyranny over these States.—To prove this, let facts be submitted to a candid World. Then go on & give 27 reasons for their declaring their Independancy (as that) He (the King) has forbidden his Governors to pass Laws of pressing importance.—He has called together Legislators at places unusual, uncomfortable, and distant from the depository of their public Records, for the sole purpose of fatigueing them into compliance with his Measures.—He has dessolved Representative houses repeatedly, for opposing with manly firmness his invasions on the rights of the people.—He has made judges dependant on his own will alone.—He has erected a multitude of new offices (officers) & sent a swarm of officers to harris our people & eat out their Substance.—He has kept up among us in times of peace standing Armies &c.—for imposing Taxes on us without our consent. For taking away our Charters & altering the form of our Governments,—for declaring the Parlament to be invested with power to legislate for us, in all Cases whatever.—He has made War against us.—He has plundered our seas, ravaged our coasts, burnt our towns & destroyed the lives of our people.—He has at this time transported large armies of foreign Troops to compleat the works of Death & desolation &c. In every stage of these oppressions we have petitioned for redress in the most humble terms, which has been answered only

1776 In Congress. only by repeated injury &c &c to the No of 27 Reasons.
July 4 — 1776 We therefor the Representatives of the United States of America in General Congress assembled, appealing to the Supreme judge of the World for the rectitude of our intentions, do, in the name, & by the authority of the good people of those Colonies, Solemnly publish & declare, that these Colonies are and of right ought to be Free & Independant States: that they are absolved from all allegiance to the British Crown & that all political connection between them & the State of Great-Britain, is & ought to be totally dissolved: and that as Free & Independant States they have full power to levy War, conclude peace, contract alliances, establish commerce, & to do all other Acts & things which Independant States may of right do. And for the support of this Declaration, with a firm reliance on the protection of divine providence, We mutually pledge to each other, our lives, our fortunes, and our sacred honor. Signed by order and in behalf of the Congress

attest John Hancock president

Charles Thompson Secretary

Augst. Sept^{r}. & Octo^{r}. fine Season

Novr 11 uncommon fine warm Weather for 3 Weeks past & but little Raine. Winds small from the W. to S. W. & South Except 2 or 3 Days an E wind as warm as in May. — In s^{d} 3 Weeks we have had 4 or 5 very white frost's but by 10 or 11 A. m., quite warm, Evenings fine & calm; but this morning Came up a fresh raw E. wind & by 2 P. m. began to Raine. This is the first day we have seen the Gease fly, when many flocks [going] from the E. to the S. W. pas'd over us.

This afternoon was drove by at Cambridge a large drove of

BATTLE OF TRENTON.

1776 Nov 11	of Cattle & notwithstanding the unnatural War is still careing on we have a plenty of most of the Nessacrys of life: Blessed be God for those & all other Mercy's.
Nov 15	this morning sett off from my house my son for New York. Still fine Weather
22^{d}	Still fine warm Weather, but the driest time that Ever I Remember for the time of Year, Yet my Well has 13 feet & 10 Inches of Water in it, when many Brooks & Wells has been dry som time
Decr 1st	Very dry time till last Night, a plenty of Raine
4th	Plenty of Raine last night and this day. Brooks now full.
5th	fine day & W^{n}. wind & cold
Sattrday 21	N. E. Snow Storm all Day & most of the Night
Sunday a. m.	fine Day. Snow 10 Inches deep on a level.
24	fine sleding & fine Weather till the
26,	then came on a N. E. Snow Storm, P. m., Wind at East & turn'd to Raine & blew at N. & N. E. very hard till midnight
27	A fine Day
Janu^{y}. 30 1777	(We have had Cold weather for 5 Weeks past except a Day or two): this morning came on an Easterly Snow Storm that continv'd till ne'r Night & left us a fine coat of Snow about 7 or 8 Inches deep: then a spel of better Weather
Febu^{y}. 11.	A Snow Storm Came on at 8 A. m. Wind at South & gradualy back'd to E. & N. E. & blew hard & snow'd very fast til 10 at Night, so that in the morning of the
12th	we found the Snow 12 or 13 inches deep on a Level. By Letters from my Son and others from New Jerseys, we have accounts of the Success of General Washington

1777 Febu[r]. 12th ton, who with 2400 men in a Terable N. E. Storm of Snow Haile & Raine cross'd the Delaware River & atack'd on the morning of Dec[r]. 26., 1,900. Hessians & som English light horse at Trenton[1] in the Jerseys. & took 919 prisoners, kill'd & wounded about 70. in the whole 989, A number soon after taken made the whol about 1200,[2] & took 6 fine brass field pieces, 7 Standerds, a Number of fine Waggons, pork, Flower &c & 1200 Small Arms. The British light horse road off & so eskap'd: our loss did not exceed 20 kill'd & wounded.— In a Letter dated Feb[y]. 10, my son writes me The British Army are Ensurkel'd in Brunswrick[3] & are so short of provision that they are Dayly Deserting to Gen: Washingtons Army.

Febu[y] 24 Came on a Snow Storm, Wind at N. E. and blew ver hard all Day & the Night following:

25th this morning we found the snow, full 10 Inches deep in adition to what was before on the Ground, with the Wind still at N. E. & raw cold

26. a fine Day, clear & warm

28 Clear & very Cold

March 2[d] (Sabbath) Wind at N. W. & Extreem cold

5th do 6 & 7 more moderate

a

[1] This battle and capture of the Hessians was at the most critical period of the war, when the Provincial forces were reduced to 6,000 men, and the outlook was most gloomy for the Patriots.

[2] This probably refers to Princeton, where the British lost 500 men in killed, wounded, and prisoners.

[3] Washington had intended to capture the magazine at Brunswick after the battle of Princeton; but the American troops were too exhausted for more fighting. After these two victories the people generally rose in arms and beleaguered the British troops in Brunswick, cut off from their main body at New York.

1777 March 24 a fine Day, planted some peas

28th ver Cold 4 Days. It frose very hard 4 nights going

April 5th Very Cold this morning, as it has been 3 Days past, & frose very hard 3 nights past

15th this Morning I found in a paile at my back Door Ice that frose last night full half an Inch thick.

May 5th raw cold weather Still

11 very raw Cold weather Still, & this morning a white frost & it frose in a tub in my yard full as thick as a Copper

12th Snow'd in the morning fast.

13 So Cold that 'twas uncomfortable to do anything abroad. Wind N. W.

14 Mor warmer by the Winds shifting

26 very hot so as to open our Dovrs & Windows for are wind from W. to S. W.

27 Warm in the Morning & for 3 Days the Apple Trees has been as full of blossoms as ever was remembered, Aboute 9 this morning the wind sudently shifted from S. W. to E. & in 3 hours was raw Cold. Which encreasing to the 28 with som Raine in Showers it continued so Cold that we found the fire as comfortable as in March.

28 Lection Day. The General Court met in Boston. Speaker & Clerk the same as last Year; The number returned to represent the Towns &c, was 249, which is 32 less than last Year, & 28 councelors was chosen as usual

July 14 Fine Raine for 2 Nights past but Yesterday uncommon Cold, Wind about East for 48 howers. We have had Showers in plenty hether to, A prety good crop of Hay, but

1777 July 14 but the apples is like to fall short, 'tho' there was as great a blow of blossoms as ever was seen; 'tis thought the uncom. cold & frost in may hurt the buds & blossoms. Plums, Cherrys &c but very few this year.

Septr 9th This morning at 2 O'clock died the Rev^{d} Dr. Ebene^{r}. Pemberton, in the 73^{d} Year of his Age & 50th of his ministry: he rec^{d} the degrees of batcheller & master of Arts in 1721 & 1724; he spent the first Years of his Ministry at New York aboute 25 years, when an unhappy differance arose in the Church and he with his Collegue M^{r}. Cumming Asked a dismifsion, which was reluctantly granted in one day, Soon after Dr Pemberton returned to Boston, the place of his Birth & was soon chosen unanimously by the New Brick Church & Congreg^{n}; of which he died pastor after Serving his Master & the Church aboute 25 years, he left neither Wife or Child, he had bured 4 Wifes, but never had a Child, 'tho' he took care of Several.

Octo^{r}. 22 This morning & last Night so Cold that I found in a Tub in my yard Ice full 1/4 of an Inch thick. The first Night we have had so cold this fall.

28 A Cold long storm of Raine Wind E.

On the 17th Inst. Lev^{t}. General John Burgyne at Saratoga Surrendered himself and his whole army, to Maj^{r} Genl. Horatio Gates, Consisting of 5,752, when he first came with his army from Canaday he had in all 9,213, Indians included, but 3,461 [1] were before he surrendered either, kil'd

[1] The actual return of prisoners taken by General Gates, as made by him' was 3,875. Of those surrendered, about 1,600 were German troops. Burgoyne's losses, according to his own account, had amounted to 1,160

1777 Octo^r. 17th kil'd taken, or deserted, wounded or Sick, who all fell into our hands.

1778 Cambridg Febu^y. 7th Last Evening at 7 O'Clock came on a Snow Storm & raw Cold E. Wind & this morning Snows fast & very Cold Wind shifting to N. & N. W.

15 Sunday morning. Extreem cold as it has been 2 days past. Wind from N. W. to W. But about 12 at noon grew warmer the Wind vearing about 2 points from W. to S.

16 & 17 do. do.

18 do. do. til near Noon

19 fine Day, wind S. W.

This month the small-pox began to spred in Boston & numbers were Inoculated. Every thing looks dark as War &c.[1]

March 22^d (Sabbath) It frose very hard last night & blew like a herican, as it did all day yesterday; Wind at N. W. A m. P. m. at W. This morning at N. W. boath days as Cold as I can remember any for 50 Years at this season

23^d frose hard last night, but the Wind did not blow so hard, Wind got to N. this morning

30th A terable Snow Storm came on last evening & blew very hard all Night. Wind at E. & b N, this morning continues, with snow hail & raine & very Cold, & looks like the middle of Winter

Still

killed, wounded, and missing, including 73 officers, since he left Canada, and before the surrender at Saratoga. This victory led to the recognition of the United States by France, and later to the French alliance, in the spring of 1778.

[1] This was the most discouraging period of the war, and doubtless the letters from Valley Forge were not of a character to add to the hopes of the Patriots at home.

1778 March 31st Still snowing & cold, Trees & everything cover'd as in the dep's of Winter, Wind at N.

April 5th Sabbath, A. m. 8 O'Clock, Snowing fast, wind at N. It began Yesterday P. m. at 5 and snow'd all night, for this morning it was near 12 Inches deep & 'tho' the 5th of April looks like the dep's of Winter. Everything looks dark,[1] as War &c good Lord deliver us & ours from Enemies abrod, & Extortion among ourselves every Nesacry of Life is exceeding dear

May 30 a Frost last night after 2 cold Days of a West & N. W. wind, which damag'd the Corn Beens &c, cut of most of the peaches & put everything back, but a fine Season after, 'tho' everything continues by reason of the War very dear: In June Butter from 3/6 to 4/ Beef 2/ &c &c

June 24 An Eclips of the Sun as great as ever I saw. Beginning at 9h. 18m The middle at 10h 30m, Duration 2h. 30m. The sun was Eclips'd about 11 Digits. It was something Cloudy, but saw it at times very plain. It appear'd just as the New Moon does at 3 Days old. Moderat Weather. Wind aboute S. S. W. the Darkness came on the S. W. side of the Sun & pass'd off on the S. E.

25 fine pleasant morning & so nothing uncomon has yet turn'd up as some people immagin from Eclips's.

27 extreem hot & continued so for 5 days

July 3 P. m. Thunder &c 2 Evenings

4th 5 & 6 Cool

7th Extreem hot again

Gen:

[1] The winter had been bitterly cold in the South as well as in New England; the spring came on but slowly, and the army had suffered severely. Small as it was in numbers, even necessities were not obtainable.

BATTLE OF MONMOUTH.

1778 Mem^m Gen: Clinton with the Brittish army left Philad^a the 18 June and march'd throw the Jerseys, in order to get to New York, but they were atack'd by Genl Washington Lee[1] &c on the 28 Sabbath and Washington &c Lost 59 Killed & 137 Wounded, total 196.[2] The Britons as follows

248 Rank & file Killed & left on the field
4 officers do
1,255 Wounded } 'twas said the Britons drove off 63
117 prisoners } wagons of wounded men
1,572 deserted since they left philadelphia

3,196 Total loss to the Brittons[3]

July 24 Rideing with my Wife in my Chaise, from my house in Lit^l Cambridge, to Watertown, a waggon with 4 stoute Horses upon the full run came suddently upon us, & jam'd my Horse back against the Chaise, broke one shaff & [did] som other damage; but the Horses & Waggon Stopt'd so suddently that it apeared as a merical, that We nor our Horse was hurt but a trifel. Blessed be God for preserving Mercy

Aug^st 5 fine rains after a very dry time, and things look florishing

[1] Charles Lee was defeated at the battle of Monmouth, although he had 13,000 troops against 10,000. Washington found the army in full retreat on his arrival. He censured Lee, and taking command in person rallied the troops and defeated the British. Lee after this affair was tried by court martial and retired to private life.

[2] The American loss in the battle was 229, including 8 officers.

[3] The British loss was 349, but during Clinton's march to New York after the battle, his total losses from desertions, etc., have been variously estimated at from 1,500 to 2,000, all told.

1778 Augst 5 — ishing. Praise must be given to the Father of all our mercy's.

9 — Sabth Excessive hot till 1 O'Clock when a Thunder shower came on, & rain'd plentifully for 4 houers, then ceased, & began again & rained about 1 in the Night till 6 in the morni^{g}.

12 — Wednesday. In the Evening came on a terable storm of Wind & Raine which continu'd the whole night & next day, but abated something P. m. & rose again at dark & blew hard all Night the Wind from N. E. to E. the whole time with Raine. this storm blew down Trees and in many fields the corn lay flat on the Ground

26th — 3 O'clock P. m. Extreem hot, now 3 Days. —

Septr. 13th — Doc^{r}. Eliot died

Octo^{r}. 15 — I moved from my House in Cambridge (that I sold to Mr. James Foster) into my House in Boston, that I built 20 years ago.

Decr 23 — It came on cold A. m. and continued increesing. Wind N. W.

Boston — The next morning very Cold & stil increesing. Wind stil N. W. with a vapor on the Water, but little Ice.

25 — Christmas Day Friday, in the morning at sunriseing I look'd down Boston Harbor & could see no water, except a few spots call'd windholes. For the vapor was great and the Harbor as far as I could see skim'd over with Ice. I had about a gil of N. E. Rum in a Case Bottle cork'd, that stood on a shelf in the pantry, At dinner time found it froze, but two full Bottles in the case was not frose. This was the coldest Christmas that ever I remember, nor do I remember that I ever had

1778 Decr 25 had any Rum frose before in my keeping, having now kept house near 47 years. this day was clear A. m. till about noon, except very thick dark clouds in the East, but about one & two O'Clock it grew Cloudy over head, at dusk it snow'd a little fine snow.

26 But the next morning before Day the Snow Storm Came on with Wind at North and blew & snow'd very hard all day, this was as Cold a Storm as ever I remember.

27 Sabbath-day Extreem Cold, very few people at meeting, Snow about a foot deep, in Drifts much deeper,

28 Still extreem Cold in the morning & last night

29 Cold abated

30th Thanksgiveng, appointed by Congress throw oute the 13 States, this Day moderat weather; Wind S. W. and by 10 O'Clock began to thaw

1779 Janu^y 4 Fine moderat weather 4 Days past. Wind about S. W.

March 5th The Inhabitants of the Town of Boston Mett at 10 O'Clock to receive the Report of the com^te chosen on the 5th of March last to aply to a proper Gentleman to deliver an Oration on this Day to perpetuate[1] the Massacre perpetrated on the Evening of the 5th of March 1770 (See the acc^t. in this Book of s^d Evening) The Com^te Reported that they had engaged Col. Tudor to deliver an Oration on this Day & Voted to adjourn the meeting to 12 O'Clock to meet at the Old Brick Meeting house and chose a Com^te to wait on s^d Tudor to request him to be ready at the time & place. Accordingly the Councle, and a great number of all ranks of people assembled

[1] After the massacre the 5th of March was observed until 1783, when the 4th of July replaced it.

1779 March 5th sembled, when the oration was deliver'd, which took near 40 minutes: when finished there was a general claping of hands to show their Approbation. This day we had a Snow Storm which continued the whole Day. Wind from S. E. to E. Note. We had as fine moderate weather all last month as we have Known in Febuy. for many Years past. But We have now a distressing time for want of Bread. Flower has rose in price in a few Weeks past from 15 pounds to £27.10 per hundred paper money and at this day not a barrel to be got, except the Comte of the town can borrow some of the French Concle,[1] who is now in this Town, a Gentleman of good carrecector for humanaty &c.

March 18 Extreem cold last night & this morning for the time of year. We have had more Winter since this month Came in, 3 to one, than we had all the last month. Wind from W. to N. W. 3 days.

19 Snow'd all day, wind S. W.

20th Extreem Cold this morning for the time of Year. Wind N. W.

March 22d Last night Came on a terable Cold N. E. snow Storm and this morning (Monday) found it snowing & blowing very hard & fast which continu'd all day & most of the night

23d A pleasant day

Wednesday

[1] It will be remembered that the alliance with France had been arranged in the spring of 1778. The French Consul at time of the visit of the French fleet in 1778 was Monsieur de l'Etombe. An amusing account of a dinner to the French officers, at which the French Consul was present, at Mr. Tracy's house in Cambridge, when they were served with a soup containing bull-frogs in their natural dress, much to the entertainment of the guests, will be found in the "Memorial History of Boston."

IMPORTANT NAVAL VICTORY.

1779 March 24th Wednesday aboute 9 O'clock A. m. Came on another bad N. E. snow Storm which lasted till 6 p. m. more terable than on Monday last, then abated, at 9 it look'd as if we should have a fine day on the morrow, but behold, on the morrow

25th At 7 O'Clock very Cold, Wind at North & Snowing very fast. So that before 9, with one snow so soon upon what fell yesterday 'tis suppos'd upon a level to be 15 or 18 Inches deep. Now everything looks dismal. The distress for Bread is great; for by what I hear many hundreds for some Days past & at this Day have not a bit to eat. Indian meale has lately bin sold at a Dollar a quart stric measure in paper money.[1] Everything Extreem dear.

April 16th Arrived the Frigate Warren John Hopkins[2] Esq[r] Commander, who in company with the Continental ships Ranger & Queen of France took the following fleet bound from New York to Georgia, viz, Kings ship 20 Guns & 150 men, ship Maria, 16 guns, 84 men, & a privateer 16 guns 45 men, together with 3 or 4 Brigs & a schooner: Transports with soldiers, stores &c two Col[s] & a number of officers. This is the greatest thing done on the sea by Americans since the War commenc'd

18 This morning at sunrising got up & found it extreem Cold for the time of Year. Wind at W. & b N. it blew hard

[1] The Continental paper money had fallen at this time to about 20 to 1 in gold.

[2] Capt. John Burroughs Hopkins, a son of Admiral Esek Hopkins. There were seven vessels captured in all, with 200 men and 24 officers. The loss on the American side was small.

1779 April 18 hard the 1st part of the Night and this morning I found the Ice in a Tub half an Inch thick & took a Quarter of a hun'd weight & put on it, which it bore without cracking. The tub stood close under the house, oute of the wind where it was not so cold as in other places, where it froze harder. — I stamp'td on the Ground in my Garden that was all sow'd & planted & many seed up, but my foot made no impression on the Ground

19 found it had again frose hard. But the Ice in the same Tub that [contained] the Ice [which] had all thaw'd in the sun, was frose hard, but not so much as the Night before

20th Still cold: Frose hard last Night, Wind continu's at West, P. m. came round to East

21st a fine warm day

a great scarcety for Bread: gave this morning four paper Dollors for 2 small Brick Loafs, that each weight but a pound & 2 ounces, which is near 60 £ per hund^d Lawful money; Wood is allso very scarce & dear

June 10 & 11 A fine groing Season. But all the Nessaicrys of Life Extreem dear. Butter current at 3 paper Dollors a pound Beef 9/ Veal from 4/6 to 6/ milk from 3/ to 4/ per quart, all shocking

19 Still a fine groing Season

Augst 2 Still a fine groing season to Oct 31st

Octr. 27th This Day P. m. was ordained (in Kings Chapel so called) the Revd Mr. Joseph Eccle[1] to the pastoral care of the Old South Church in Boston (the Old South Meetingh^e

[1] Rev. Joseph Eckley was born in London, England. He was a graduate of Princeton College, New Jersey, and remained in charge of the Old South Church from this period until his death in 1811.

1779 Octr 27th Meetingh^s still remaining as when the Regulars left it.)

Novr 3 P. m. Was ordained over the N. North Church[1] the Rev^d. John Eliot[2] son of the late worthy Dr Andrew Eliot pastor of the s^d N. North church Boston

22 We have had fine dry moderate Weather this fall but alas extortion still prevails, Butter is lately rose from 2 Dol^s a lb. to 3, 4 & 5 & milk from 2/6 to 3 & for 10 Days past 4/ per Quart, as the late Regulating Acts is all broke throw

Decr 9 Thanksgiven day. Butter got from 5 to 6 & 7 Dol^s a pound milk to a Dol^r a quart, Beef to 10/ the best to 12/ per pound & other things in proportion. Some wreches ask'd 3 Dol^s a pound for pork and when & where things will stand Time must determine

18 About Daybreak came on A terable Snow Storm Wind E. & contin^d till P. m. 4 O'Clock. Wind got to the North & began to break.

28th A very Cold Season for 12 Days past 28th P. m. Came on a snow Storm, Wind at East and about 9 O'Clock it blew exceeding hard & snow'd fast

29 Last night a terable Storm & snowing fast till near 12 the Wind Shifting to the Norward

A

[1] The New North Church was first located on the south side of Hanover street, about midway between Fleet and Commercial streets, in 1714. The Church was at first a small building of wood, replaced by a more substantial structure in 1802. It was from this church, in 1720, that the minority of twenty-four withdrew on the Rev. Peter Thacher being installed as minister. The twenty-four seceders built the New Brick Church, and later united with the Second Church.

[2] Rev. John Eliot was born in Boston 31 May, 1754; graduated at Harvard College in 1772; received degree of D.D. from Edinburgh University in 1797; one of the founders of the Massachusetts Historical Society; died 14 February, 1814.

1779 Decr 30 A great snow fell last night & this a. m. warmer & foggy

1780 Janu^y 1st last evening the wind freshened up about West & blew fresh and this New Years morning extreem Cold Wind at West.

2^d Sabbath day Extreem cold, but allmost calm till 7 or 8 in the evening, when it began to blow hard about N. E. as we suppos'd, it being very dark and by 9 it blew a near Hurecan & began to snow & a terable storm continued all night. In the morning we found it snowing very fast, a full tide, which continu'd till 12. Then began to abate, the wind shifting more to the North & Extreem Cold.

4th Still cold and now we have 3 snows on the ground, suppos'd to be on a level 3 feet deep. In the morning stil, clear, & extreem Cold. At noon clear and pleasant

6th In the morning found it Snowing & very Cold & by noon another snow 6 Inches. So now 4 bodys of it.

7th this morning another snow falling & very cold. Wind from N. to N. W. two or 3 days past. Milk at a Dollar & half a Quart & wine measur: Such is the advantage taken of those unhappy Distressing times, almost everything in proportion.

8th Clear & Extreem Cold. On observation & inquiring hear & think the snow is 4 feet deep on a level, and 'tis commonly said there has not been so much snow at one time on this part of the Globe for 20 Years and excepting a day or two, it has been Extreem Cold a month past

9th Still Cold. This Sabbath just after day light a Fire

broke

1780 Janu^{y} 9th broke oute on Hancocks Wharf[1] & burnt down a large Warehouse at the lower part with many Ships Sailes & Riging, but did no other damage it being almost calm, several large Ships laying near.

10th A little moderated

11th found it snowing fast, this is the 5th Snow since the 18th of last Month

12th little moderated & plesant

13th Extreem Cold again

20th Thursday. Still Extreem Cold. People say as cold as ever they remember

21 Extreme Cold last night, the Shovel-fire & Tongs was cold as they stood in the Chimney Corners

22^{d} Cold

23^{d} Sabbath. Extreme Cold. The Harbor frose as far as we can see

26 Continues Still extreem cold

28th Extreem Cold. Wind W & b S., Very clear Sky fair Weather 14 Days past

29th Satter^{y}. Yesterday clear & little wind till 7 in the Evening came on a hard Gale of Wind about N. W. and blew hard til near Day. At Sun Rising allmost calm & Extreem cold & clear, Little Wind about W. & as cold as ever I remember

30th a little moderated

31 At sunrise extreem Cold. Wind ab^{t} N. W. til about 11 then Shifted to West

Febu^{y}. 1st Wind S. & b West. Something moderat

2 Very Cold at sunrising, little Wind, about Westerly. Yesterday

[1] Hancock's Wharf is now a part of and on the north side of Lewis' Wharf, though they were formerly distinct.

1780 Febuʸ. 2 Yesterday & toDay the Harbor as far as we could see was frose up

3ᵈ Wind S. pleasant & warmer

4 Cold

5 clear & Cold, a little moderated

6ᵗʰ A fine pleasant Day

7ᵗʰ at daybreak came on a N. E. Snow Storm & by 7 O'Clock snow'd very fast

15ᵗʰ More Moderat. P. M. Misty: evening began to Raine fast & continued Raining & blew hard the former part of the Night & found the snow in the morning, that had lain on the Gound 4 or 5 weeks much shrunk. This raine Came Seasonably for many Wells in Town were dry, as we have had but little Raine for near 2 months, but a great deal of Snow.

Febʸ. 17ᵗʰ A fine warm day as it has bin now 4 or 5 Days past

March 1ˢᵗ We had prety good Weather the most of last month.

12ᵗʰ Sabbath Day came on a terable Easterly snow Storm

23ᵈ Very Cold this morning. Wind N. W.

29ᵗʰ Leap Year. very Cold yesterday. Wind at W & blew hard all Day & frose hard last night & very Cold this morning

Apˡ. 3 very Windy & very Cold for several Days past & frose hard 5 nights going. Wind from W. to N. W.

17ᵗʰ This morning found it very Cold & Snowing very fast. Wind fresh & squally from N. to N. N. West & dismal to look abroad, for everything has within 10 or 12 Days rose. (fresh Fish excepted) to a Shocking prise. Pork 7 Dolˢ, Beef from 4 to 5 Dolˢ a pound, Butter & hogs fat to 11/ and so on

Bread

THE DARK DAY

1780 Ap^l^. 17 Bread is beyond all. Very corse dark flower part Rye is at 120 £ that is 400 dol^s^ per hundred

19 About 7 this morning came on a great N. E. Storm with Raine & kept encreesing till 12, the time of high Water & caus'd a very high Tide, which did much damage to the Wharfs

23 Very Cold this morning & evening and as cold an April as ever I remember. Scarce 1 warm Day since it came in

30 Mrs Marg^t^. Coolidge, who lived in my Family 23 years till lately, she, on her Daughters being marred to Mr Copp, removed from us to her s^d^ Daughters: But alass on the Sabbath of April 30–1780 she was suddenly removed from us all. Being at Meeting boath parts of the Day, as well as her feeble Constetution admitted of, and just before the last prayer ended P. m. She without a sigh or Groan dropt'd ded on the Floor of my pew where she stood just by my Wife. The Congregation all in a great surprise at so Sudden a Death. — Thus suddently departed our good & beloved freind from this World of troble, to the Realms of Everlasting Bliss, There to receive the Rewards of a, wel don good and faithfull servant, enter thou into the joy of thy Lord. God grant that this may be the happy lot of all related & conserned for the dear departed above said. She was deacently Bured in my tomb[1] May 4th Thursday

May 19th Friday just before 11 O'Clock came on an uncommon darkness, so that before 12 it was so dark that Trades-men

[1] This was No. 13 in King's Chapel Burying-ground, at the south-east corner of the chapel.

1780 May 19th	men & others left off work, not being able to see what they were doing, at 12 numbers lit up Candles in their Houses, the darkness increased so much that people when they dined could not See to cut their Victuals, but by the lights on their Tables, and so it continued till near 4 when it grew a little lighter, and by 5 the Vapors & lower Clouds began to move from the S. W. to wards the N. E. There was till this movement a glin of light in the Eastern & S. En Horison, but it was soon darkened as the Vapor & Clouds Settled over it, when it look'd, where the glin was a little before, very dark & thick, in short there was at noon & for 3 or 4 hours some appearance of midnight at noon Day. In the evening before 9 O'Clock it was very Dark. by 9 & at 10 so extreem dark, that perhaps it never was darker since the Children of Israel was freed from Egiptian bondage. Many people was much frightened; the moon was about the full, so it could not be an Eclips of the Sun[1]
June 6	for a month past but little Raine.
On the 8	a fine Shower & 2 evenings past do.
July	but little Raine Thunder or Lightning
Augst 24th	Extreem hot 2 Days & last Friday & Satterday the same
25	At 6 P. m. yesterday a fine Shower & a little Thunder & Lightg & this morning a cool Easterly Wind
Dry Time } 28	Still extreem hot
Octobr.	The greatest part of this month fine weather
27	Friday A. great Eclipse of the Sun began about half after

[1] This dark day has been attributed to burning forests at the West. The same effect has occurred in recent times.

1780 Oct[r] 27 after 11 O'Clock, middle about one, Quantity 11 digits odd &c.

Octob[r] 25th (Wednesday) General Election, agreeable to the New Constitution of this State. The Day was ushered in by the ringing of all the Bells, firing of Cannon &c &c. The Members Chosen by the several Towns came to the State House; Subscribed the Declarations, Oaths &c &c. Then a com[te] examined the Returns of the several Towns in the State for a Governor when it was found by A great Majority that his Excelency John Hancock Esq[r] was elected Governor and the Honora[le] James Bowdoin L[t] Governor & one of the Senators (but did not accept of either). After all the serimoneys (which brought it to 3 O'Clock P.m) was gone throw, the governor & boath houses went to the Old Brick Meeting House[1] where an Excelent Discourse was delivered by the Rev[d] Dr. Cooper[2] from Jeremiah 30th part of 20th & 21st verses: And their Congregation

[1] The building referred to, also called the First Church, was built in 1712, to replace the wooden church on the same site, burned in 1711. It stood until 1808 on Cornhill, now Washington street, next south of Sears Building. The first location of this church was opposite the east end of the Town House, or Old State House, on King street, now State street, on the south side. It was moved from there in 1640. In 1808 the society moved to the corner of Summer and Chauncy streets, where they remained until 1868, and then moved to the corner of Marlboro' and Berkeley streets.

[2] Samuel Cooper, brother of William Cooper and son of Rev. William Cooper, was born in Boston, 28 March, 1725, graduated at Harvard College, 1743; chosen assistant pastor of Brattle-street Church, with Dr. Colman, 31 December, 1744; ordained 21 May, 1746; A. M. Yale, 1750; S. T. D. Edinburgh, 1767; elected president of Harvard College, 10 February, 1774, but declined; chaplain to the General Court of Massachusetts, 1758–70 and 1777–83. Founder of American Academy of Arts and Sciences, and first vice-president, 1780–3; died 29 December, 1783.

1780 Octob[r] 25th Congregation shall be established and their Nobles shall be of themselves and their Governor shall proceed out of the midst of them. After which they went to Faneuil Hall, amidst a very larg Concourse of people, where a grand Entertainment was provided & 13 Toasts were drank. John Avery[1] Esq[r]. Jn[r]. was chose Secretary. Deacon Caleb Davis[2] Esq[r]. Speaker (one of the members for Boston) An[w] Henshaw[3] Esq[r]. clerk. The number of Counsellors was 40, and Representatives from all the County's 11 in Number was to the amount of 224. Viz[t] For Suffolk 29 (Bos[n] sent 7) Essex 31. Middlesex 32. Hampshire 34 Plymo[h] 13. Barnstable 8, Bristol 14. York 9 Worcester 33 Cumberland 4 Berkshire 17. In all as above 224

Nov[r]. Sett in the first day with a Violent Snow Storm, a high Tide & did much Damage to the Wharves &c and several Vessels as we heard afterwards was cast away.

17th Another Storm Raine. Wind at N. E. as it was the last Storm

Dec[r]. 31st With the Year I Resign'd my Office as a Treasurer in, or to the 2[d] Church[4] in Boston. This office as well as the Deacon's I held for many Years, in the time of Mess.

[1] John Avery died in 1806, was graduated at Harvard College in 1759, the son of John Avery, a Boston merchant. He survived his father only ten years.

[2] Caleb Davis was born in Boston in 1747, was Selectman and Overseer of the Poor for several years; was several times Representative and Speaker; was Deacon in Hollis-street Church; died in 1797.

[3] Andrew Henshaw graduated at Harvard College in 1768, and died in 1782.

[4] Called the North Church, also the Church of the Mathers and the Old North Church. It was located at North Square, and first regularly occupied in 1650.

1780 Decr. 31st Mess. Welsted & Gray's Ministry, till their Death and in Dr Pemberton's time. And when the two Churches, the Old North & New Brick United into one,[1] under the pastoral care of Mr. Lathrop, the Church & Congregation Unanimously chose me Treasurer again. In which Office I served to this Day. But as Old Age came on (being in my 72d Year) & being in Chhs servise near 42 Years, I finaly Resigned, on the 3d Meeting on the affair, when the Society still requested me to keep the money & Books. I thanked them all for the Respect they had shewn me for so many Years. & finding me determined to quit, They Unanimously Voted me their Thanks for my faithful services (as they called them) for so many Years. Deacon Greenough Accepted of the Treasurer Ship till next May.

1781 Febuy 8th We have had a favorable Winter & but little Snow. But this Day Friday the 9th in the morning We found it extreem Cold with a Vapor on the Harbor. The first we have seen this Winter. Wind fresh from W. to N. W. & very Cold all Day

Satterday 10th In the morning We found it Snowing Very fast & fine. Wind about N. N. E. & very Cold & a high Tide. The Docks full of Ice drove in by the storm: the Snow continued falling very fast till sun down, then seas'd.

11th Sunday. A fine Day but bad traviling. The Snow fell 12 Inches upon an everage. Some say 18

Monday 12th In the morning found it extreem Cold, but clear. Wind about W. & b S. but almost calm. The Harbor skim'd over with Ice as far as we could see.

Moderate

[1] The Old North Church, being of wood, had been used for fuel by the British troops during the siege in the winter of 1775–6.

1781 Febuʸ 13 Moderate & good sleding

14th A fine warm day. Wind S. S. W. and no want of the nesacarys of Life, but our own produce stil dear

March 7th This morning We found it blowing hard at N. E. Which increased to a Storm & before 12 it Snowed fast & very raw Cold

8th In the morning We found it Snowing & still Cold & suppose it Snow'd all night for it was 12 Inches deep on a level. But by 12 O'Clock it began to clear away & the wind got to the Northward & by 3 to N. West and the sun shining made it plesent after the Storm.

March 30 Friday, being at a Town Meeting where I was Moderaʳ we was broke up by the Cry of Fire &c, when we soon found a large House, quite down to the Northend of Boston all in flames and the Wind at N. E. blowing very high & a number of Wooden Houses & barns being near & to Leavard & the Flakes of fire blowing to a distance & lighting on many houses which ketch'd on fire made the prospect before us Dredfull. The house was all consumed in 2 howers and the Town preserved by the Goodness of God in a wonderful manner. Many people did not run to the fire as formerly, but kept wetting their houses to leavard.

April 2 a cold Storm of Snow & Raine, Wind at N. E. The latter part of March was very cold & Stormey

13 Sill very raw Cold. This morning it began to Snow by ½ after 7. very thick till after 9 a. m.

14 a fine clear morning but very Cold at Sunrising & frose hard last night.

May 3d Fast Day Throw the 13 States. We have had a Cold backward Spring: but 2 or 3 Days past something warmʳ.

Tuesday

THE BRITISH SURRENDER AT YORKTOWN.

1781 May 8 Tuesday came on a N. E. Storm with Raine

9th Storm Continues & last night it blew a very great Storm & a high Tide, (being just after the full Moon) which did much Damage to the Wharfs. A great deale of Raine fel in 2 Days & nights & very cold for the Season

11th A fine clear morning & a white frost

June & July A fine groing Season. Every nesacary plenty, but very dear as the paper money Depreciated, Till at last the old paper Emision, so called, by the middle of May [had] sunk so, as that it did not pass, which threw the Trade into confution.

Augst 6th 4 O'Clock P. m. Extreem hot since 8 or 9 this a. m. Just came oute of my Garden, where stood a Vinegar Cask, with a Quart Bottle as usual in the Bunghole. I took the Bottle in my hand & felt it so hot with the Suns Shining on it that I could not hold it ¼ of a minute.

8th This is the 3d Day of Extreem heat.

Octr Good Weather & every Nesacary, plenty except hard Cash, for the paper Curency stop'd about the 1st to 10th July[1]

Octr 26 This morning A hand Bill as follows.

Capt Lovett from York-River (Virginia) Chesapeake Bay brought us the Glorious News of the surrender of lord Cornwallis & his Army, prisoners of War to the Allied Army[2] under the Command of our Illustrious Genl Washington

[1] Although not generally current after the middle of May, some persons appear to have accepted the paper money for two months longer.

[2] The allied army contained about 7,000 French and 9,000 Continental troops and militia.

1781 Oct[r] 26 Washington & the French Fleet Commanded by his Excelency the Count de Grasse. A Cessation of Arms took place the 18th Octo[r].[1] and the 19th the Allied Army took possession of York-Town. By this Glorious Conquest 9000 of the Enemy,[2] including Seamen &c fell into our hands with an emence quantity of Warlike Stores, Viz[t] Brass cannon &c 95 Iron do. Swivels &c 169 from 1 pound to 24 pounders: Shot &c &c in proportion: Regimential Standards, German, 32, British 41, Total 76.

Octo[r]. Fire Arms 5,743 Muskets with Bayenots, 915 without bayenots 1136 d[o] damaged, Carbines pistoles &c &c &c a vast number, wagons, Horses &c &c. Provisions 276 Bar[s]. Flour 520 bags Bread 96 bbs Beef 365 bbs Pork 361 firkins Butter, 58 Cask Oatmeal 596 bbs Peas, quantity 2,985 bushels, 13 Casks liquers, 26 Bags Coffee, 20 Bags cocoa, 50 bags Salt, 3 hog[s] Sugar, 3 Casks Vinegar, 3 Jars Oil, 29 Barrels rice, 1 cask Reasons. A List of Vessels taken, or destroyed at s[d] York: the Charon 44 guns, Guardalop 28 Foway 24, Bonetta 14, Vulcan a fire Ship, a privateer of 20 Guns. 2 Duch prises; near a 100 Transports & other Vessels. The naval prisoners Exclusive of those belonging to the private Transports and other Vessels are 840, perhaps as many more not mentioned. A marvilous Affair in the course of Providence. In Octo[r] a great number of Young

[1] The armistice was on the 17th October. After forty-eight hours of negotiations, the troops marched out of Yorktown and laid down their arms.

[2] There were 7,073 prisoners taken, besides losses before the surrender amounting to 586 on the British side.

1781 Octo[r]	Young Children died, but about the midle of Nov[r] the distemper abated.
Dec[r] 13th	A general Thanksgiving throu' the 13 Provinces. every necessary plenty and provision cheeper that it has been for 3 Years past.
15th	Fine Weather & good sleding 3 Days past
1782 Jan[y] 12	We have had prety good weather till last Evening came on a Snow Storm & this morning it blew hard & very Cold. Snow'd fast, Wind from N. E. to E. A. m., P. m Wind vear'd more N.
13	Sunday morning cold. Snow 10 or 12 Inches deep very few people at meeting
14	Plesent
15	In the morning very Cold with a large Vapor on the Harbor. The first we have seen this Winter.
16	This morning extreem Cold. The Harbor froze over as far as we could see by noon, & P. m. clear & moderate
17	This morning again extreem Cold. Wind W. & b S. The harbor as yesterday morning skim'd over with Ice, which yesterday P. m. the Ebb Tide carred off
18 & 19	A Thaw
21	Grew Cold
22[d]	In the morning extreem Cold. Wind W. & b N. A large Vapor on the Water
23 & 24th	In the morning We found it snowing fast & very Cold. Wind N. E. blew fresh & suppos'd it [continued] all night for we found it Snowing in the morning & very Cold. Wind at N. till about noon [when] the wind vear'd to the West, cleared up & we had a fine P. m. Snow 12 Inches deep on the last snow

This

1782 Janu^y^ 28	This morning Snowing as large flakes as I ever Saw. Suppose it Snowed most of the Night, as it was at 9 A. M. 8 Inches deep on the Old snow.
29	Extreem Cold. Wind W & be N
30th	do but little wind at W & be S.
Febu^y^. 1st	This is the 4th Day of extreem Cold & this morning till 10 O'Clock I don't remember ever to have felt it Colder: About 12 it began to moderate & Calm.
9	for 4 or 5 Days past prety moderat, til 11 this Day. the Wind Came on fresh at N. W. & Continu'd very Cold at sundown and all night till Sunday Noon, when wind got to S. W. &
Monday 11th	a. fine Day
12	about 8 last evening came on a Gale at W. grew Cold & this morning found it extreem Cold Wind West
13	fine moderat Day til sundown. Wind came on fresh & Cold
14th	Extreem Cold in the morning
22 & 23d	fine & pleasent
24th	Extreem Cold. A Vapor on the Water in the morning
25	Clear & extreem Cold. The Harbor skimmed over 3 mornings with ice
April 26	for 10 Days past we have had very raw, cold uncomfortable Weather. The Wind from N & b E. to N. E. without vearing 3 points for 10 or 12 Days and an abondance of Raine
May 2d	fine Weather. S. W. Wind. Grass thick & growing finely, but the
3d & 4th	again Cold & raw. Wind at N. E. & more Raine
June 22	Extreem hot Weather for 3 Days, but this evening some black Clouds came over with Thunder & Lightning

1782 June 22 ning & a smart Shower but still continued very hot. But Sabbath morning

23^d^ found the ear much colder & but little Wind at east: but at noon the Wind came again to the South & was soon extreem hot; But about the Middle of Sermon P. m. som black Clouds came up from the West, and on a Sudden there came a terable gust of Wind, that made the People, Doors & Windows Tremble: and in about half an hower a smart Shower & some Thunder: and at times fine Showers till near sundown, When the Sun broke oute before it sett & for a Quarter of an hower as fine & large A Rainbow as I ever Saw apear'd and all nature appear'd most Charming, with a S. W. Breaze.

24 a fine Clear Day. Wind at West

June 26 A fine Day and this Day I have ben marred just fifty Years to the beloved Wife of my Youth with whome throw the goodness of God to us & ours, We have lived the whole Time very comfortably & at this Day are So.

Jubilee We have in our youth full Days had Six Children 3 Sons & 3 Daughters, but our two Eldest Sons Died at Sea, John our first born in his 23^d^ Year & James in his 17th. We have had 12 Grandsons & 4 Granddaughters, but we have lost by Death 6 Grandsons 2 of them Men grown vizt. Tomey Stanly & Capt Willm Thompson; Granddaughters all living Except one. As this day compleated the fifty years of our marrage (and in all that Time We have never ben absent 5 Weeks at one Time from Each Other. We kept a Day of jublee and made

1782 June 26 Jubilee — made an Entertainment for our Children & their Children (all that was Living). And a Lovely sight & Day we had of it, to see so many of a family to gather on such an acation. Blessed be God for it. If our first born John had ben living he would have bin in his 50th year. Our oldest Daughter Mary present in her 48th year.

August 8 — An extreme Dry time very little Raine for 5 Weeks last past This day was Lanch'd at Clark's Yard[1] the French Packet Brig called the Dragon, built for the King of France. She is to mount 18 carrage Guns: from the Day her Keel was laid till Lanch'd was but 5 Weeks & 3 Days. This was the 1st vessell ever Lanch'd in Boston under French collors, with a Number of Green Bows round the Quarters &c according to the French mode. A great Number of Spectators, a fine Lanch &c &c.

Augst. 9 — Extreem hot & dry, but just before 4 O'Clock P. m came up a Cool East Wind this morning soon after Sunrising we had the Larm Guns fired and by 4 P. m. I saw 10 large French ships in Sight. Som came to anchor in Nantasket road. Some in King road. 2 Came up near the Town

14th — One of the 74 Gun Ships came to saile & by some bad manigement got on Lovell's Island Point just after high Water, where she was lost, but the People, Stores &c was saved.

19th — This morning came on a fine Raine after an extreem dry time

Still

[1] Clark's Ship-yard was at the foot of Clark Street at the North End.

1782 Septr. 8 Still very dry & two Days in this Week vizt. 5th & 7th Extreem hot. Wind S. S. W.

Septem^r 11th A. m. Still hot & Dry; but before 10 came on a fine Shower of Raine for aboute 4 howers, this changed the arc & the 12th Wind about West & cool

The Summer just past has bin the dryest for 20 Years past vizt. 1762 when there was two dry summers following. But this Drouh is cheefly in & to the Westward of Boston for 50 miles, but to the Eastward & in the Southern States we hear that they have had a fine Season.

25th Continues extreem dry (tho' yesterday P. m. we had a Shower of half a ower). This Day my Well was Dry, the 1st time since I dug it, 20 Years ago this Month.

Octo^r. 1 Stil Extreem Dry Weather til this morning, came on a stidy Rain for 4 or 5 howers

30 & 31 A plenty of Raine

Novr. 2^d. Clear & Cold, this is the first morning we have seen any Ice this fall

On Sunday Novr. 10 A. m. I went to the Chapple[1] in Boston to hear Mr. Freeman[2] Read prayers & preach. His Tex was Search the Scriptures. The Old South people met with the Church people. In the forenoon the Ch^h of England Service was carred on & P. m. the Congregation^l way and boath Worship^d togather with the Ministers, tho' Mr Freeman was not Ordain'd, as he could not go to England in those unhappy times of War with England. And the Reason of the 2 Congregations meeting in this way was, that when the British troops had possession of

[1] King's Chapel, corner of School and Tremont Streets.
[2] Dr. James Freeman.

1782 Nov[r]. 10 of the Town, they cruely tore down all the inside of the Old South Meeting house to exercise their Horses in, So that when the people that where forss'd oute of Town return'd they was oblig'd to borrow the Chapple to meet in. The Chapple people then went to Trinity Church[1] as Doc[r]. Canner[2] their Minister went off with the British troops, when they where destitute of a preacher for some years, as the War continued between England & America. But about this time the Chapple people and said Freeman Agreed and with the Old South people met & Worshipt'd as aforesaid, and to me it was Agreeable to see former Bigatree so far gon & going off, and God grant that for Time to come boath Churchmen & Desenters may live in peace & Love

Dec[r]. 6 about 5 O'Clock this morning We saw a Ship of 300 Tons, just off the end of long Wharf, on fire & by 6 was all in a blaze, the Wind at West & fresh, she was soon consum'd with her cargo of masts spares &c. This week arived in Boston from Providence R. Isl[d] the French Troops, som say 3, som 4 or 5 thousd in order to Imbark for the West Ind[s]., on board the French fleet now in the Harbor & in Nantasket Road.

10 Jemmy Thompson came to live with us for som time in order

[1] Trinity Church was first opened for services in the old wooden church, in 1735, on the corner of Hawley and Summer streets. In 1823 the granite church was built on the same site, and destroyed in the great fire of 1872. Rev. Addington Davenport was the first rector.

[2] Dr. Henry Caner carried off with him 2,800 oz. of silver service, and all the records and vestments of the church, which were never recovered.

1782 Decr. 10 order to go to School in Boston & on the 11 Inst went to Mr. —— School in State Street.

11 We have had moderat Weather all this fall & Winter except a Day or 2 & Snow is Kept off in & near Boston. provision plenty but dear, partly owing to a Number of Troops & Strangers in & about Town

24 French fleet Sailed about 1 O'Clock from Nantasket Boston Harbour &c with a number of Troops on Board.

25 This morning about 2 O'Clock a fire broke out at the North Mills[1] in Boston, which entirely consumed them with a Number of Stores & Stables near, a 1,000 bushels of Grain, Cocoa, Chocolate &c &c where burnt, with all the Cocolate Works; allso horses & hogs. The fire made a terable blaze, but as the Wind was light, about Northerly, carried the Flames & Sparks over the pond,[2] the Safety of the Town under providence was preserved.

31 Yesterday P. m. & last Night came on an Easterly Storm of Snow, & Raine in the evening, but this morning a pleasant Wind West

1783 Januy 7th this Evening it blew fresh at West & grew Cold

8th In the morning We found it clear & Cold

9th Cloudy & Extreem Cold the Harbor skimm'd Over with Ice as far as we could See

Jany. 10th Friday morning. See it Snowing Small snow & very fast that continued all Day. Satterday morning Still Snowing but not so much as yesterday, & suppos'd it snow'd all Night as the snow was 18 Inches deep & stil Cold,

[1] These mills stood near Endicott Court at the North End of Endicott Street, a little south-west of the Gas Works.

[2] The Mill Cove then occupied all the land now traversed by North Margin Street on the east, Haymarket Square and South Margin Street on the west, and portions of the streets crossing these.

1783 Jany. 10th Cold. the sun broke out by 11 but Clouded up again by one

15 again Extreem Cold

17, 18 & 19 Warm, a Janu^{y} Thaw

last Sabath 12th Our Ch^{h} began to Sing P. m. Doc^{r} Watts's Hymns[1] as per a Vote of the Church: We had a Subscrip^{n}. for a N^{o} of Books that we gave to the poor which was put into Col. Proctors[2] & my hands to distribute

Febu^{y}. 1 Extreem Cold yesterday & last Night & this morning

3 Yesterday Sunday & Candlem^{s}. Day. Extreem Cold, & this morning stil extreem Cold & the Harbor cover'd with Ice, Wind stil West & clear Weather.

Satterday March 1st We had a very hard Storm Wind about South all Day, from 10 to 3 in the afternoon it blew Extreem hard, but moderated before Night.

Monday 3^{d} prety Cold: & about Sundown thear apeared in the Clouds an uncommon Redness boath in the S. W. & N. E. for 15 or 18 minutes, So firy that many people was surpris'd but nothing uncommon the Night or Morning following.

10 Monday Yesterday P. m. in Sermon time a very dark Cloud came over Attended with a heave Gale of Wind about West, grew Cold, the Wind Continu'd blowing very hard all Night: in the Morning found it extreem Cold for the time of year, it frose hard (in the shade) all Day

11th We found it extreem Cold in the morning & a great deal

[1] Deacon Tudor had given $500 to encourage good singing in the Second Church.

[2] Colonel Edward Proctor, a Boston merchant, one of the committee appointed to regulate prices in Continental money.

PEACE PROCLAIMED.

1783 March 11th	deal of Ice made last night, but the Wind abated and more to the Southward, but continues Cold.
22	A. M. fine Weather, but P. m. came on very raw Cold
23d	Sunday morning found it snowing fast & by 8 O'Clock the Snow was 9 Inches deep, but it Clear'd away by 11 & prety moderate.
April 11th	we have had a Dry time for 3 Weeks past
12	a considerable Raine Wind E.
13	Clear & very Cold for the Season frose hard last Night
18	very warm yesterday & this Day for the Season
19	In the morning the Wind sprung up at West & coninu'd riseing & by 11 O'Clock it was very Cold for the season
Apl 23d Peace	At Noon a Cessation of Arms[1] against Great Britton was declar'd from the Balcony of the Townhouse.
May 1st	We have had as dry an Apl. as ever I remember, but yesterday P. m. We had a small Shower & do. at 9 in the Evening
June 1st	Yesterday & this Day (Sabbath) very cold for the time of Year. Wind from N. E. to E
	The later part of June & the begining of July as fine a growing Season as ever was known
July 4th	(Friday) The Anniversary of our Independance was observed in Boston. The Court at 11 O'Clock was escorted by the Train of Artillery to Docr. Coopers Meeting, when Docr Cooper made an elegant address to

[1] The first treaty, where the British Government acknowledged the independence of the United States, had been signed on the 30th November, 1782, when hostilities ceased. The final treaty of peace was not signed until 3d September, 1783.

1783 July 4th to the Assembly and a well adapted prayer, then an Anthem [was] Sung and the Solemnity concluded by an Oration delivered by Dr John Warren[1] at the request of the Town.

24 Allmost every thing plenty and a fine groing Season Extreem hot, Wind about S. W. A plenty of provision

Augst 24 Sabbath. extreem hot yesterday & toDay. Wind S. W.

Septr. A plenty of Raine and all the Nessacarys of life.

Octor. Ditto

Novemr. 1st Last Night about 11 O'Clock came on a good deal of hard Thunder & sharp Lightning and all the Week past verry Raw Cold Weather with a greate deal of Raine til this afternoon the weather broke with the first Quarter of the Moon: for 6 Weeks past we have had as much Raine as ever I remember in sutch a space of time.

Monday Decr. 29 Died Docr. Saml. Cooper in the 59 Year of his age & [40th year] of his minestry, his Corps was caried into

1784 Jan 2d the Church, where a Sermon was Deliver'd by the Revd. Mr Clark[2] to a great concourse of people

April 17 A very Cold Day. Wind at N. W. & be W. & Snowed all Day. We have had the longest & Coldest Winter that has bin since 1741

August & Septemr. We have had a Dry Summer & Fall but no great want of anything, as the Navigation is all free, a fine Dry fall

[1] Dr. John Warren was born at Roxbury, 27th July, 1753; graduated at Harvard College in 1771; studied medicine with his brother General Joseph Warren, and in 1773 removed to Salem. After his brother's death at Bunker Hill he joined the army as surgeon, and remained until 1777, when he took charge of the military hospitals in Boston until the end of the war. He died 14th April, 1815.

[2] Rev. John Clark, D.D., was born in 1765; graduated at Harvard College in 1774; made associate with Dr. Chauncy in 1778 over the First Church; died 1807.

1784 August & Septem^r^. fall & moderate. By the middle of Novem^r^ Wood was Cheeper than in July last. That I cant learn that any one ever remembered before.

Novr. 26 this morning We found a smart Gale at E. with a plenty of Rain that Encreas'd to a terable Storm by 11 and

High tide comes into my gard^n^ brought in a high Tide over all the Wharfs, concequently som Thousand pounds damage in sugar Salt &c, but before 1 P. m. it was allmost Calm, before 2 a small brease came on at S. and by 4 a smart Gale at S. W. that continu'd til bedtime.

27 A Moderat Cloudy Morning with a fresh wind at S. W.

1785 A Cold backward Spring til May; in June & July a fine groing Season and Butter & many things begin to fall. Money, vizt. hard Cash is very Scarse, owing to multitudes in Town & Contrey runing into Dress &c and Cash being Shiptd to England &c for vain Superfluetys

Aug^st^ 12 This P. m. I atended as a paul-holder to Deacon Greenough's Funeral, he was in his 76 year. — And alass this Day at 12 Deacon Brown Died. He was in his 77 year. boath Brother Deacons & Acquainted from our youth and to the last we held a Brotherly Love together.

1786 March 24th this Day I went to Trinity Church, a. m. to hear Bishop Seabury from Connec^t^ preach & Conferm a number of Men Women & Children, his Text from Acts 8th & 17 V's The 1st Bishop I ever saw: he preach[ed] & confirm'd soon after a number at the North Church Call'd Christ Ch^h^

May 7th I Rezined my office as Treasurer [2] to the 2^d^ Church in Boston

[1] The following extract is from the last sermon preached in the Second Church by Rev. Chandler Robbins, on 11 March, 1844, just before the church was abandoned: "At the head of these stands Deacon John Tudor,

OPENING OF THE FIRST CHARLESTOWN BRIDGE.

1786 May 7th Boston and the Chh Chose Deacon Ridgway in my room. The Chh voted me Thanks for my past Services &c. then chose a comte to examin my accounts: the comte mett on the 10th May

May 10 When sd Comte was pleas'd to say, they Wished Every Officer's Accounts &c was as well settled as mine. I paid the Ballance in my hands to Treasurer Ridgway: Rect given at the Settlement in the Chhs. Book at the close of the account. J. Tudor

31 Lection Day, I went down to Charleston Ferry P. m. and saw the last pear of the Bridge settled, & the Guns fired for joy on the acation, as allso for the Election.

June 17 This day Charles River Bridge[1] was finish'd, when a vast concourse of people passed over: There was two Tables of 320 feet sett up on Bunker's hill, the place where the Battle was foug't with the Brittons this Day 11 Years, on the Day Charleston was burnt. This Day of festivity & joy was Kept so as to Entertain 800 Gentlemen; the Governor's &c &c was present. 13 Tosts &c was drank &c &c. Sutch a Concourse of people,

a man of no less sincere piety than sterling honor; prudent in his affairs and systematic in his arrangements. His labors for the good of the society during his own day were various and indefatigable. Nor was he unmindful of those that should come after him. Nearly all the most valuable records of the church and society during the eighteenth century were fully and carefully kept by himself. If it were not for his careful and untiring pen nearly the whole of the ministry of Welsteed, Gray, and Pemberton would have been to us but little better than a blank. He was also a pecuniary benefactor of the society, and treasurer for about forty-two years." See Robbins' "History of Second Church," p. 199.

[1] This was the lower Charlestown bridge close to Copp's Hill.

1786 June 17 people, Carriages &c I never Saw at one Time before: Said Bridge is 1503 feet long encluding the abutments and is the greatest peice of Work ever don in Emerica. For the first pier of the Bridge was drove on the 14th June 1785 & the Bridge completed on the 17th June 1786 12 mo & 3 Days. The greatest depth of the river from the upper floring 46 feet 9 Inches. Small part 14 feet at high Water: The breadth of the Bridge 42 feet & Ornamented with 40 Lamps, which make a Sparkling Show in the Night The town & Contrey soon found the Advantage of this Bridge.

1787 March The Winter past has bin long & to many distressing, the money very scarce & but little Business going on.

April 16 My Grandson Wm Savage[1] went to Mr Tilston's[2] School

April 20 (Friday Evening) About Sunset a Fire broke out at the South part of Boston and within about 3 hours was never Equalled in this town, excepting in the year 1711 & 1760. It raged on both Sides the Street 10 or 15 buildings being in flames in a few minutes, til about 100 buildings were destroyed; sixty of which were dweling houses, many Elegant ones. Among them was a hansom meeting house. Subscriptions & Colections was set on foot to relieve the unhappy sufferers & large sums obtained.

1788 Novemr 11 Last evening our two Granddaughters Jane & Betsy[3] Savage

[1] William Savage was the elder brother of James Savage, the famous genealogist.

[2] John Tileston, who presided over the Eliot School for more than sixty-five years. The school was on North Bennet Street at the North End.

[3] Elizabeth Savage married John Cooper in 1791.

1788 Novem^{r} 11 Savage went to Notels Iland[1] to board with Mr. Williams their Dear mother being Dead & the House broke up &c

12 Just at 11 came in a mesenger & told me that my Farmhouse at Lynn was Burnt down yesterday P. m. in the time of the Terable Storm we had. So uncertain is all below the Sun. The Lord gives & he takes away. Bless^{d}. be his Name &c &c.

1789 May 23 P. m. We had the good News Conferm'd of our Daughter Tudor's being Safely Delivered of a Son[2] at Dorchester

22^{d} We have had a Cold May &c, til this Day, but throug mercy everything plenty, but money his hardly to [be] com at.

1790 April Very Cold for the Season on the 17, 18 & 19 till Sumer began. Summer most things plenty but money, but money Scarce.

Decem^{r}. Sett in with Rain & snow, Cold &c lasted all the month.

1791 Janu^{y}. 1 A very Cold Snow Storm that lasted all day, at ev^{g} broke

2^{d} Clear & very Cold, the Snow from 3 Snow Storms in Drifts is in some places from 4 to 6 feet high upon a Level as the Contrey people say 'tis

July 5 P. m. My son Wm Tudor's right leg was broak at Notamy by the kick of a horse & brought safe to his house in Boston on the 7th

1792 In June we by a Letter from our Grandson Cooper[3] who Lives

[1] Noddle's Island.

[2] This was James Tudor, who died 9 August, 1797.

[3] John Cooper was born in Boston, 13 December, 1765; was educated at the Boston Latin School. He removed to Machias, Me., in 1790; was High Sheriff of Washington County, Me., for thirty years, and Treasurer of Washington County for six years; was Brigadier-General of

W. Tadorp.

1792 Lives at Machias had the Agreeable news of our Dear granddaughter Betsy's safe Deliverance of a Great Grandson born the 6th inst who was soon baptized by the Name of John Tudor [1] by the Revd Mr Lyon June 6th 1792 the Great Grandson J. Tudor was born about 3 P. m. on a Wednesday in 1792 he was Wean'd June 6 1793, which he took finely. A Lovely fine Boy as good Natured as ever I saw, Bessed be God for all. We might by this time have had a Number, But alass our oldest Grand Children has been Dead some time. Lord preserve all.

Aug. 30. This day my grandsons Wm Tudor [2] & Wm Savage were both

Massachusetts Militia from 1803–11; in 1812 was chosen Commissioner to deliver to Congress the electoral votes of Massachusetts; in 1816 was a delegate to the convention, at Brunswick, for the separation of Maine from Massachusetts; in 1822 he removed to Cooper, Me., where he died the 18th November, 1845.

[1] John Tudor Cooper died, 22 March, 1812.

[2] William Tudor was the eldest son of Colonel Tudor, born in Boston, 28 January, 1779; was prepared for college at Phillips Academy, Andover, and graduated from Harvard College in the class of 1796. He was sent to Paris on business by John Codman, Esq., soon after graduation, and after his return to Boston, again sailed for Leghorn, and made a tour of Europe for pleasure and study. In 1805 he was one of the founders of the Anthology Club, out of which grew the Boston Athenæum, of which he was one of the founders. In the fall of the same year he went to the West Indies with James Savage, in connection with his brother Frederic's business of the ice trade; and in 1807 went to France on the same business. In 1810 he went again to Europe, as agent of Stephen Higginson, Esq. In 1815 he founded the "North American Review," which is still in existence, and edited it for many years. He was the originator and one of the founders of the Bunker Hill Monument. He delivered the Phi Beta Kappa oration in 1815, and the 4th of July oration, in Boston, in 1809. He published, besides a "Life of James Otis" (his most noted work), "Letters from the Eastern States," and "Gebel Teir." Having been appointed consul for Lima, he left Boston, in November, 1823; was charge d'affaires at Rio in 1827, and died there of yellow fever, 9 March, 1830.

1792 Aug. 30. both inoculated for the small-pox. Broke out the Beginning of Sepr. both did well. Mercy. Mercy.

Memorandum of the great small-pox in Sepr. 1792

At a meeting at Faneuil Hall on Monday Octor 8th 1792 Report was made to the Town that last Week the Selectmen and Overseers of the poor with a number of Clergy and other Gentlemen visited all the Families in the several Wards in this Town in order to obn a particular Account of the Small pox &c As follows

Whites by Inoculation		8,804	died	158
Blacks	Inod	384	died	7
dito	Natural way	18	do	6
Number from the country		1038		
Removed out of Town		262		
Subject to infectn		221		

It is to be observed that tho' the number is said to be 221, in those are included many children &c

The town voted Unanimously that the Selectmen be requested to take all legal Measures for Removal of persons who do not belong to this Town

By Order Wm Cooper Town Clerk

1793 Oct 1st Warm with a S. W. Wind so small that the flys was as Troublesome as ever. Ditto on 3d day as on the 1st

4th Do

5th At 11 fine Weather do on ye 9th & 10th

7th Calm ordinary. Fine Weather for the Season. do the 8th & till ye 10th extraordinary for the Season. The flys very troublesome Still. So Warm at 11 'tis more

1793 Oct. 7th	more like Summer than October. Governor Hancock lays Dead. He Died on the 5 Inst morning
11th	Warm, extreordenery Warm, Clear &c for the Season
14	Governor Hancock Bured this P. m. The Bells began to Toll at SunRise for ½ an hower. A great perade &c this P. m. of Guns &c &c. Flys very Busey at Noon

SO END

THE MEMORANDUMS.

COPY OF DEACON JOHN TUDOR'S WILL.

From Probate Records, Suffolk County, Mass., Vol. 93, p. 291.

I John Tudor of Boston in the County of Suffolk and Commonwealth of Massachusetts Esquire, now near eighty three years old, but being through the goodness of God in good health and understanding and memory do with my own hand write and through this now ordain this to be my last Will and Testament. And first I order my just debts and funeral expenses to be paid as soon as may be after my decease. — Also I give & bequeath to my beloved Wife Jane Tudor with whom I have happily and comfortably lived more than Sixty years being married on the 15th of June 1732. To her I say I give the House I now dwell in and all its appurtenances together with the use of all my plate that may be in the house excepting what I have before given away, and all my Household furniture during her life, but she shall sell none, and I desire and direct my executor hereafter named to keep the said House and Fencing in good repair; and I do further give my said Wife an Annuity of one hundred and fifty dollars per year to be paid her quarterly 37 & ½ dollars out of the interest arising from my bonds and mortgages; — Also I give to my Daughter Mary Thompson (now a Widow during) her Widowhood the Sum of Fifty dollars to be paid her quarterly 12 Dols & ½ I give to my Daughter in law Dil[a] Tudor my sons wife two hundred Dollars to be disposed of as she thinks proper. also I give to each of the 9 Children of my deceased Daughter Eliz[h] Savage five dollars to be paid to them upon their arriving at the age of twenty one,[1] or day of marriage; and in case of the death of either of them the said Legacy to be equally divided among the living Brothers & Sisters. I give devise and bequeath to my only son Will[m] Tudor Esq all the rest residue and remainder of my estate Real Personal & mixed and I do hereby constitute him my said Son the Executor of this my last Will. and

[1] This legacy of $5 was increased to $500 each by William Tudor, the executor, who inherited the bulk of the estate.

I prohibit any Inventory being taken of my estate to be lodged in any office. And I do Earnestly recommend to my Son the tender & affectionate care of his aged Mother (but I think I need not give this caution as he has always been a dutiful child) this may bring a blessing on him and his Amen, as to my Tomb No 13 with my name on it at the old burying ground at and near the S. E. corner of the Stone Chappel in Boston I say and direct that it shall not be disposed of but kept in the family for the use of my Family till time and death shall be no more — I hereby in case of my Son and Executor's death do appoint my Daughter in law my Son's wife Dil^a. Tudor[2] to be the Administratrix of this my Will. — As I have left my Wife as above the House &c together with the quarterly payment of 37 Dols & ½ both which may be a genteel and comfortable maintainance but I leave all as above & before written to the discretion of my Son and Executor; In a particular manner as my Grand Children may turn out And I hereby make void all other Wills before made by me:

In Witness whereof I hereto set my hand and seal this sixth day of August in the year of our Lord one thousand seven hundred and ninety-two, — at the writing of the above I am in health and good circumstances today but I Know not what may be on the morrow much less what may be next month or year; I may possably live to spend all; If so my Heirs &c must be content to do as well as they can. — I give to my grandson J. H. Tudor my picture in a large four square guilt frame drawn above forty years ago with the paper on the back of it — And further as I being old may die soon I hereby give to my said Son Willm all my four Desks and Glass case as it now hangs full of papers and desire him to take them all away to his House as soon as may be after my Funeral is over, together as they now stand, with all that may be in them as Bonds &c

John Tudor and a Seal

Signed Sealed & Delivered in presence of us

Henry Roby
Thomas Lewis
Thomas Lewis Jr.

([2] See page 110.)

[2] Delia Jarvis, the wife of Colonel William Tudor, born 18 Nov. 1753, was the daughter of Elias Jarvis, Jr., and Deliverance Atkins. Her father died early and her mother married for her second husband Capt. J. Young. She belonged to a tory family, but her sympathies appear to have soon turned to the patriots. She had considerable literary ability, and was one of the social celebrities of old Boston after the Revolution. She is said to have learned the Italian language after her eightieth year. The following lines were written in 1843, when she was about ninety, in memory of the battle, for which the monument, in which her eldest son had been much interested, was just then completed at Charlestown. She died a few months after at Washington, 7 Sept. 1843. The lines published 24 June, 1843, in the "National Intelligencer," are as follows:

Ecclesiastes, Ch. 1. V. 9.

Had it been thine, great King! on earth to stay,
And note the dawnings of this peerless day,
To future years those words would not resound —
That "Nothing new beneath the sun is found."

Mute as in Heaven, no party strife takes place,
Though adverse thousands crowd those names to trace
Who on this hallowed spot in martial pride
Fought for their country — conquered, bled and died!
On Freedom's sons devolve the vast domain,
Who unimpaired the sacred trust sustain.
Wilds that no mortal footstep then had pressed,
A home invites the sufferer — the oppressed.
No rigid rules depress his daily toil:
Lord of himself, lord of the cultured soil,
A happy future opens to his view:
Rich culture springs where tangled forests grew,
And children's children in succession rise
To bless the barque that gained these distant skies.

VII

MEMOIR OF WILLIAM TUDOR.

William Tudor, born 8 April, 1750, was the youngest child and the only surviving son of Deacon John Tudor, the two elder brothers having died at sea. He was fitted for college at the Latin school on the South side of School Street, kept by Mr. John Lovell, and entered Harvard University in August, 1765. His room-mate in college was Theopholous Parsons, afterwards Chief Justice and the friendship there begun continued through life. William Tudor graduated at Harvard in the class of 1769, with considerable reputation as a classical scholar.

At the age of twenty-one, in 1771, he entered John Adams' office to study law. The condition of Public affairs in the Province of the Massachusetts Bay was at this time critical. The Provincial Congress had met for the first time, October, 1765, after the passage of the Stamp Act, nine of the Colonies only being represented. The embargo on British goods had been adopted by all. The mob had destroyed the houses of Oliver and Hutchinson in Boston and in many of the other Colonies had the same riotous proceedings been carried out. The enforcement of the Stamp Act at this time would have doubtless led to an open rupture, but it was repealed in the following year because the king's party were not yet prepared for open war. But in 1767 a similar act was passed and a powerful fleet and army sent to enforce it. Boston was then considered the hot-bed of rebellion, and the presence of the great body of British troops sent to hold the town could lead but to one result. First the exchange of insults between the troops and townspeople culminating finally on that bitter March day of 1770 in the Boston massacre.

John Adams was the foremost lawyer of the day, not so eloquent as J. Otis, nor so much of a tribune of the people as Sam. Adams, but with a calm mind watching events and always ready to give his legal opinion and the weight of his position to the patriot cause. It was just before leaving Mr. Adams' office

Errata in line 6 for "Theopholous" read "Theophilus"

that occurred the event at the end of 1773, so momentous for all the Colonies since called the Boston Tea Party. While this destruction of the East India Company's tea in Boston Harbor was the act of a mob, it was without doubt countenanced and probably instigated by the patriot leaders and supported by the public opinion of a majority of the citizens. It was for this reason that the law closing the Port of Boston and the succeeding acts annulling the charter were passed at the very time the young lawyer was opening an office for himself. The prospects were certainly gloomy in the extreme. All business had ceased in the town of Boston, and where there was no commerce, there was little occupation in the law. All men knew and felt that war was in the air, and while no overt act had been done, both sides were waiting, and private quarrels were put aside. William Tudor had now passed the age of twenty four years; he had completed his studies, had been entered at the bar, and his father probably considered that he had done enough for him. The son had, however, secured the esteem and friendship of Mr. Adams, while in his office, which lasted all his life, and was the cause of the followlng long letter written in his favor to his father.

BRAINTREE, July 23, 1774.

Dear Sir: —

You will be surprised I believe to receive a letter from me, upon a matter which I have so little right to intermeddle with as the subject of this, I am sensible it is a subject of very great delicacy; but as it is of equal importance to your own happiness and that of your only son, I hope and believe you will receive it, as it is really meant, as an expression of my friendship both to yourself and him, without any other view or motive whatever. Your son has never said a word to me, but from what I have accidentally heard from others I have reason to believe that he is worried and uneasy in his mind. This discontent is in danger of producing very disagreable effects, as it must interrupt his happiness, and as it may and probably will, if not removed, injure his health, and by discouraging his mind and depressing his spirits, disincline him to, or disqualify him for his studies and business. I believe sir, you are not as sensible as I am, of the difficulty of a young gentleman's getting into much business in the practice of the law. It must, in the best of times and for the most promising genius, be work of time. The present situation of public affairs is such as has rendered this difficulty tenfold greater than ever. The grant from the crown of salaries to the judges, the proceedings of the two houses of Assembly in relation to it, and the general discontent throughout all the countries of the Province, among jurors and others concerning it, had well-nigh ruined the business of all the lawyers in the government, before the news of the three late acts of Parliament arrived. These acts have put an end to all the business of the law in Boston. The Port act of itself has done much toward this, but the other two acts* have spread throughout the Province such an apprehension that there will be no business for courts for some time to come, that our business is at present in a manner at an end. In this state of things I am sure it is impossible that your son's income should be adequate to his necessary expenses, however frugal he may be, and I have heard that he complains that is not. The expenses for the rent of his office, for his board and washing, must come to a considerable sum annually, without counting a farthing for the transient charges, which a young gentleman of the most sober and virtuous character can no more avoid, than he can those for bed and board. So that it is absolutely impossible but that he must run behind hand and be obliged to run in debt for necessaries, unless he is either assisted by his father, or leaves the town of Boston and betakes himself to some distant place in the country, where, if his business should not be more, his expenses would be vastly less. I am well aware of the follies and vices so fashionable among many of the young gentlemen of our age and country, and if your son was infected with them, would never have become an advocate for him, without his knowledge, as I now am, with his father. I should think the more he was restrained the better. But I know him to have a clear head and an honest, faithful heart. He is virtuous, sober, steady, industrious, and constant to his office. He is as frugal as he can be in his rank and class of life, without being mean. It is your

* Mr. Adams was at this period nearly forty years of age. He had been for a long time the most prominent lawyer in Boston and had taken from the beginning a quiet but active interest in all the contests between the crown and the people of the Colonies. His friendship and good offices for William Tudor were continued during his life, as their constant correspondence shows.

Errata in line 3 for " be work " read " be a work ".

peculiar felicity to have a son whose behaviour and character are thus deserving. Now there can be nothing in this life so exqisitely painful, to such a mind so humiliating, so mortifying, as to be distrusted by his father — as to be obliged to borrow of strangers, or to run in debt and lie at mercy. A small donation of real or personal estate, made to him now, would probably be of more service to him, than ten times that sum ten years hence. It would give him a small income that he could depend upon — it would give him weight and reputation in the world — it would assist him greatly in getting into business. I am under concern lest the anxiety he now struggles with should prove fatal to him. I have written this without his knowledge, and I don't propose ever to acquaint him with it. If you please you may burn this, only I must entreat that you believe it to flow only from real concern for a young gentleman whom I greatly esteem.

I am your friend and humble servant,

JOHN ADAMS.

To JOHN TUDOR, ESQ. CAMBRIDGE.

What was the result of this letter the writer of this does not know, probably it had some effect on the old Deacon, but events were fast shaping themselves in a way to give occupation of a serious nature to all the patriots. Just two months after the writing of the above letter by Mr. Adams, the Provincial legislature was dissolved by proclamation of General Gage, but meeting on their own account organized themselves into a Provincial Congress without the Royal Governor's assistance. This was in itself almost a declaration of war, as the now independent congress was rapidly arming and training troops and gathering warlike munitions. Actual war came on quickly, and in less than seven months the first blood was shed in open battle at Lexington, and within three weeks Ticonderoga was taken by the Patriots After Lexington the siege of Boston was begun, and amongst others shut up there was William Tudor. Why he stayed in the town, a patriot amongst the British forces is a simple story. He was in love with a Tory maiden who was so far from any sympathy from her own country that her family still continued to use the taboed tea, the selling and buying of which was considered then little better than a crime in the town of Boston. This young woman Delia Jarvis is even said to have given the forbidden drink to the British troops returning exhausted from the Lexington skirmish. Open warfare was, however, too much for the young patriot lawyer, and soon after the siege of the town was begun by the Provincials, and before all the boats had been seized by General Gage, he managed to escape by way of Point Shirley to the Provincial lines where he joined the besieging army at Cambridge, on the 12th of May, 1775. He found, however, a curious means of visiting the woman of his choice, who had now moved to Noddle Island (East Boston) probably because the city was not only uncomfortable on account of the many troops, but besides a dangerous residence. Like another Leander William Tudor swam across from the main land to the Island, carrying his clothes on his head, and returned in the same way after his visit. He was always a fine swimmer and diver and when a boy is reported to have jumped from the bowsprit end of a frigate, whence none of the officers dared to follow him.

The gathering of the Provincial forces about the town of Boston and their efforts to fortify the surrounding hills led to the battle of Bunker Hill, and the fearful slaughter of the British troops. General Gage had a taste of what the Provincials could do in war, and he never again ventured to attack their entrenchments. The Provincial Congress proceeded rapidly with the organization of the army, and William Tudor was elected Judge Advocate General of all the forces, with the rank of Colonel, on July 29th, 1775, having been already appointed to that office by General Washington on the 13th, doubtless owing to the good offices of John Adams, and perhaps other friends. This position he retained for about three years, going with the army to New York, and afterwards to the Jerseys. Serving all through that period of profound discouragement to the Patriots, starving with them at Valley Forge, and receiving little or no pay. After the surrender of Burgoyne there was much trouble between the prisoners and their guards. The English troops of that day were overbearing and insolent in the extreme, and although prisoners they appear to have continued much the same actions towards their captors as they were in the habit of following towards the people of the various towns where they were quartered. They had a particular contempt for the Americans, because they were Provincials, and they considered them socially inferior. This same tone, more or less prevails in England today, and though not so common there as in India, Egypt and other conquered countries, is shown to all foreigners, and explains why the French and other nations of Europe hate the English nation with a deep and lasting hatred. No doubt the American officers and soldiers resented this sort of treatment, and when the same thing came from their prisoners, they were not particularly patient. Colonel Henley was one of those who believed that a prisoner was bound to behave himself with common decency to his superiors, and on receiving unusually insolent language from an English corporal, and finding ordinary words of reprimand of no avail, he struck him with a gun which he had taken from one of the guards, wounding him with the bayonet. This probably had a good effect, probably a whipping, or close confinement on short rations would have been more effective. The result, however, was somewhat remarkaable. General Burgoyne charged Colonel Henley with "the most indecent, violent, vindictive severity against unarmed men and intentional murder." These charges were not sustained, however, at the court martial ordered to be held.

At this late day it seems all a trivial incident, but was made much of at the time. General Burgoyne hoped probably to make capital for himself out of the affair. It at all events varied the monotony of prison life. Portions of Colonel Tudor's argument (he had been deputed to defend Henley) have been preserved. The following extracts seem the most striking:—

"This erect countenance which they boast of, leads them to looking down upon the rest of the world, though not always with impunity. Britain is feared because she is powerful. What pity it is that a native cannot be just as well as gallant. Less pride had prevented the dismemberment of her empire, had saved the blood of thousands and real magnanimity had ere this arrested the hand of destruction from the heads of men whose greatest fault, once the glorious fault of Britons, is the love of freedom."

"But," says General Burgoyne, "Colonel Henley's conduct had a great effect upon his guards: he was known to be no friend of the British soldiers (sic?): he had himself wounded one, and ought therefore to be considered as an accomplice in every outrage which took place." If this reasoning is conclusive by the same logic the General himself is an accessory to all the murders perpetrated by the ferocious bipeds the savages, who accompanied and disgraced his army last summer. Ought it to be said that because these black attendants knew that General Burgoyne did not love Americans, that therefore he would be pleased at the butchery of the nerveless old man, defenceless female and infant prattler? because he hated 'rebels,' he therefore influenced the Indians to massacre that young unfortunate, the inoffending and wretched Miss McCrea!"

The latter portion of this speech is said to have brought tears to the eyes of General Burgoyne. A characteristic remark of Colonel Henley after this trial was in requesting his defender to shoot him because in the use of the words at his trial that he "was a man of passionate and impetuous temper" his defender had ruined him in the estimation of the woman he loved. This trial of Colonel Henley was in January, 1778. The French had after the capture of Burgoyne decided to recognize the united Colonies and take an active part in the war for their independence. Though much fighting was to be done, the darkest days of the struggle had passed away, and the whole of New England was hereafter freed from the presence of British troops, or any contest of importance.

Colonel Tudor, having married early in 1778, Delia Jarvis, whose Tory training had probably given way to her affection for him, now thought it best to retire from his legal services to Washington's army, and devote himself to domestic life and the practice of his profession. This was rendered the more necessary by the absolute want of pay, which did not allow a man in service to contribute anything to the support of his wife and children. His resignation was accepted with favor by General Washington, and he retired with the rank of Colonel.

Judge Tudor soon after his marriage, opened a law office in Boston, and had a considerable practice. In those days it was the general custom for law students to learn their profession in the office of a prominent lawyer, and amongst those who became afterwards distinguished in their profession, who studied in Judge Tudor's office, were George R. Minot, afterwards Judge, Fisher Ames, Isaac Parker, afterwards Chief Justice, and Josiah Quincy. There appears to have been plenty of business at the office to support the growing family. Judge Tudor was commissioned a magistrate in 1781; was a representative in the legislature from 1791 to 1796; a senator for Suffolk County from 1801 to 1803. At the death of his father, Deacon Tudor in 1796, he inherited about forty thousand dollars in real and personal property. At that time this was a considerable estate. He was now considered one of the wealthy men of the community, and decided after the settlement of his father's estate, to give up his law practice and make a long-desired journey to Europe. He was at this period, the father of eight children, six of them living. The oldest, William, was at Harvard College, being about 18 years of age, and the others had passed the age of infancy and could best be spared for a time their father's care. The affairs of the Colonies had progressed with satisfaction since the long war with Great Britain practically ended with the surrender of Cornwallis in the autumn of 1781. The Constitution had been adopted. Vermont, Kentucky and Tennessee had been added to the original 13 States, and the long administration of Washington was drawing to an end.

This journey comprised a visit to London, Devonshire where his father was born, and thence to Paris just recovering from the wreck of republican institutions and only waiting for the strong hand of Napoleon, to re-establish order and then sacrifice the people and her institutions to his ambition to become a second Charlemagne. It was during this visit to Paris that Mr. Munroe was recalled on the change of administration from President Washington to President Adams. The Americans in Paris, including Col. Tudor, joined in an address to the retiring minister censuring the Government for his recall. It is needless to say that this action was not only unwise, but was a thing which would naturally be resented by the Government at Washington, and those taking part in it could hardly expect much consideration in future from those then in power, or any succeeding administration. The return journey was made through the Netherlands and Holland. After his arrival in London the American minister, Rufus King, presented him to the king George IV., when the following incident is related to have occurred. As this occurrence has been already twice published it can do no harm to repeat it here. The surname of Tudor is not very common and probably no one of the name had ever been presented to the king before. The name at any rate struck him and he exclaimed: "Tudor, what, one of us?" And receiving the information that Col. Tudor had recently come from France, a country just then not resorted to by the English people, the king entered into a long conversation on the condition of affairs in that country, the opinion of the people, etc., much to the annoyance of Lord Galloway, who had many others to present. when at last growing impatient, he exclaimed: "His Majesty seems so deeply engaged with his cousin that he forgets what a number of persons are in waiting to be presented!" The king, however, continued his conversation until his curiosity was satisfied.

It was not long after his return from this foreign journey that he decided to invest a part of his estate in that portion of Dorchester Neck, called Nook Hill, believing that this land lying nearest to the Town of Boston would eventually be of considerable value. This land was, it is true, separated from Boston by flats overflowed at high tide, but the available portion of the original peninsular was already nearly filled up, and it seemed reasonable to suppose that this unoccupied land so near the centre of the town would soon be needed for residences. Had this purchase remained quiescent it would doubtless have proved in time a good investment. His house property on Queen street, now Court street, had already improved greatly in value, being very close to the active business centre of the town. Boston was growing very fast and was increasing rapidly in wealth and was then the leading commercial place of the country. Some time after this Dorchester purchase Joseph Woodward, also a large landowner who may be considered the forerunner in those great land speculations, which have proven so disastrous of late years, conceived the plan of separating this outlying portion of Dorchester from the rest of the town; connecting it with Boston by a bridge and annexing it to the larger place. The scheme looked promising and Col. Tudor, Harrison Gray Otis, Jonathan Mason, Gardiner Greene and others amongst the most substantial citizens of Boston were interested in the project and made large purchases of land. Though strongly opposed in the Legislature by the town of Dorchester, a bill was passed annexing South Boston and the four persons mentioned above were also made the incorporators of a bridge company. On the passage of these two acts the value of the lands in South Boston advanced to ten times their former value and had the original owners sold their property then, no doubt great profits would have been realized. Col. Tudor, however, having invested largely in the bridge company, entered with the other owners upon the improvement of the property, grading, building breakwaters, etc. He also built on his own land a block of four brick houses, only one of which was ever rented, for the paltry sum of $120 a year. The people of the south end of Boston now fearing that the new bridge, which was to be built from Federal street, would injure their own property, managed to get the bridge located beyond their own land at the Neck, so that people were obliged to go nearly to Roxbury to get to South Boston. Anyone can anticipate the result. The bridge was built at a cost of $56,000. No one went to South Boston. The bridge never paid expenses and was sold many years after for $3,500. Five years after the bridge was finished there were only 250 people in South Boston. In the year 1807 Col. Tudor, probably satisfied with the South Boston investment, then in the full tide of apparent prosperity, went to France with his wife and daughter and was afterwards joined by his eldest son. Napoleon was then at the height of his prosperity and France was greatly changed since the former visit. The imperial court was conducted with great state and Col. Tudor and his family were frequently entertained by the Empress Josephine. His old intimacy with the French officers of the Continental Army was renewed and this visit to France, which lasted for a year, was probably most agreeable. He returned, however, to find ruin. His property had become all involved in the South Boston undertaking and he was ruthlessly pursued by his creditors. His second son, Frederic, had embarked in the ice trade to the tropics in 1805–6, and the early ventures had proven a total loss and had doubtless added to the complications of his father. They were both persecuted in every way by their creditors, being often arrested and even imprisoned. Col. Tudor now resumed the practice of the law with more or less success. He now received a magistrate's commission throughout the Commonwealth. He had been already Representative from Boston and Senator from Suffolk county, also Commissioner of Bankruptcy in 1801–2. He was afterward Secretary of State of Massachusetts for the years 1809 and 1810, and was Clerk of the Supreme Court from 1811 until his death on July 8, 1819. He delivered the Boston Massacre oration on March 5, 1779, after his return from the army, and the oration before the Cincinnati Society, of which he was vice-president, on July 4, 1791. He was on friendly terms and correspondence with many of the leading men of his day, which was the most interesting period of the Nations history. Two or three of these letters which have been already published, but are not very accessible, are included here.*

* The writer of this sketch is indebted for many details to the memoir written by William Tudor for the Massachusetts Historical Society, of which his father was one of the founders.

XVIII

From General Washington to W. Tudor, Esq.

Mount Vernon, August 18th, 1788.

Sir:—I have just received your friendly letter of the 26th of July, together with the History of the Insurrection in Massachusetts and cannot delay to return you my thanks for these tokens of your regard. Though I have not yet had time to look through the book, from the interesting nature of the subject and the judicious manner in which it seems to be handled, I anticipate considerable amusement and information. The apology for the publication at the present time is well conceived and forms a just discrimination between the circumstances of our own and some other countries. The troubles in your State may, as you justly observe, have operated in proving to the comprehension of many minds, the necessity of a more efficient government. A multiplicity of circumstances, scarcely yet investigated, appears to have co-operated in bringing about the great and, I trust, the happy revolution that is on the eve of being accomplished. It will not be uncommon that those things which were considered at the moment as real ills should have been no inconsiderable cause in producing positive and permanent national felicity For it is thus that Providence works in the mysterious course of events, "From seeming evil still educing good." I was happy to hear from several respectable quarters, that liberal policy and federal sentiments had been rapidly increasing in Massachusetts for some time past: it gives me additional pleasure to find that labor is becoming more productive and commerce more flourishing among the citizens. If I have formerly approved myself inclining to subserve the public interest, by fostering youthful merit, I shall now claim to be credited, when I assert that my cordial desires for the happiness of the republic and the prosperity of its friends are by no means diminished; and particularly when I add that, with great esteem, I am, sir,

Your most obedient and most humble servant,

G^o. Washington.

W. Tudor, Esq.

* This letter referred to an account of the Shay's rebellion by Judge Minot.

XIX

From General Knox.

Head Quarters, Morris Town, 4th May, 1777.

Dear Judge:—

I received your favor by the post, for which I thank you. The arrivals at Boston amply make up the loss at Danbury, which was very great. It was a bold push if they thought the people would have opposed them, but I believe they were led into the secret by their good friends the tories, who have uniformly deceived them; they paid a full Lexington price for the pork and beef, and that at a time they could ill afford it. Reports say that you are to be attacked at Boston by General Burgoyne with 10,000 Germans and 3,000 British. This may or may not be true, but you ought to be prepared; piers ought to be sunk between the Castle and Governor's Island, and batteries erected at the north part of the town. But I am fearful that the good opinion which my countrymen have of their harbour will prevent them from taking the only method to secure the town. General Howe still threatens Philadelphia, but our force is now so respectable that we dare defy him to put them into execution. Pray with me the prevailing sentiments and news.

I am, dear sir, yours hastily,

H. Knox.

Colonel W. Tudor.

INTRODUCTORY NOTE ON THE TUDOR GENEALOGY.

The Welsh and English genealogy here given is derived from the sources named. The descent of Deacon John Tudor from John Tadore of Penscoyd through Roger, Thomas and William, though not proved beyond a doubt, is based upon the following: His father's name was William Tudor, and his grandfather's name was Thomas Tudor. The family seal which has been handed down and the seal on the old letters, bears John Tadore's arms. It is known that his father died not long after his birth, and before middle age. The conclusion seems reasonable that he was sixth in descent from John Tadore. The arrangement of the American descendants has been as far as possible by families. As there were only two of the Deacon's children who have left descendants, there should be no great difficulty in following them. The members of the first family of children are given in Roman numerals. The others are given in ordinary figures. The figures in brackets at the side of the name indicate merely the number each has in their respective families. The figure at the end of the Christian name indicates the generation. The Christian names in brackets after the name are the ancestors of name of Tudor; b. means born; d. means died; S. P. means without issue. No attempt has been made to give any of the titles, or college degrees, or other honors. Only the designation by which they were commonly known as Colonel, Doctor, etc. The editor is greatly indebted to

From the Herleian Manuscripts containing the Heralds Visitations for the County of Northampton, 1615-18.

1187 fo. 28.
1188 fo. 11.
1553 fo. 11. b

Arms
Or a lion passant sable, charged on the shoulder with a Martlett between three annulets of the second.

John Tadore of Penscoyde, Co. Flint, Wales.
Married the daughter of Edward Lloyd, of Yale, Co. Flint, Wales,

ARMS. Paly of six argent or gules, a bordure sable, charged with eight besants.

had 5 sons:

1, John Tuder,
2, Ralph Tuder,
3, Juan Tuder,
4, Edward Tuder,
5, Roger Tudor, of Watlington, in Co. Oxon, married Margaret, daughter of Hamlett Hassold, of Nantwich in Com. Cestriae, had one son:

Thomas Tudor

Married 1st the daughter of Walter House, of Emitforth in Com. Cestriae, had one son:
Mathew Tudor.

Married 2d Dorothea, daughter of Edward Fowler of Tillesworth, Co. Bedford, had one son:
Thomas Tudor.
[Thus far the Herald's report.]

His son (as supposed) William Tudor, married Mary, and had one son:

Deacon John Tudor,
born between Exeter, Devonshire, and Topsham, 18 Sept., 1709 (O.S.), was brought by his mother, at 6 years of age, in 1714-15, to Boston, New England.

Errata in line 1 for "Herleian" read "Harleian" and in line 9, for "or" read "and".

Mrs. Rogers, Richard Sullivan, Esq., George H. Richards, Esq., and Mr. Hays Gardiner, for kind assistance in procuring family records, and particular thanks are due to Frederick Tuckerman, Esq., of Amherst, for much information regarding the Cooper branch of the family.

It was the intention to have given a short memoir of Frederic Tudor, the editor's father, and his first struggles with the ice trade; but this properly belongs to a work by itself. There are, besides, reasons not necessary to explain here why the contemplated work has been abbreviated. It is doubtful now whether the copies of portraits of three of the Deacon's grandsons mentioned in the introduction, can be done in time, as well as a copy of Deacon Tudor's portrait, and a picture of his old house at Nonantum Hill, owing to objections raised by the custodian of the papers which delayed the publication. The notes to the diary and the memoir of Colonel Tudor were fortunately finished, as well as a copy of the Deacon's will for the present volume. This being the editor's first serious literary work he hopes that any errors may be treated leniently.

W. T.

AMERICAN DESCENDANTS.

Deacon John Tudor[1] of the Second Church in Boston married 15 June 1732 (O. S.) Jane Varney b. 23 Feb. 1714 he died 18 Mar. 1795. She died 23 Sep. 1795

Their children were six, all born at Boston, Massachusetts

I John[2] bap. 25 March 1733 (O. S.) d. at sea 29 Oct. 1756
II Mary[2] b. 17 Nov. 1734 "
III Jane[2] b. 30 June 1736 "
IV James[2] b. 19 Mar. 1740 " d. at sea 11 Oct. 1756
V Elizabeth[2] b. 31 Mar. 1745 "
VI William[2] b. 28 Mar. 1750 "

VI Colonel William[2] Tudor (John[1]) married Delia Jarvis
5 March 1778 b. 18 Nov. 1753
He died 8 July 1819 She died 7 Sep. 1843
at Boston at Washington D. C.

Their children were eight

1 William[3] b. 28 Jan, 1779 d. S. P. at Rio 9 Mar. 1830
2 Delia[3] b. 21 Nov. 1780 d. at Boston 22 Nov. 1780
3 John Henry[3] b. 13 April 1782 d. S. P. at Philadelphia
4 Frederic[3] b. 4 Sep. 1783 28 Jan. 1802
5 Emma Jane[3] b. 10 Mar. 1785
6 Delia[3] b. 8 Jan. 1787
7 James[3] b. 22 May 1789 d. at Boston 9 Aug. 1797
8 Henry James[3] b. 8 April 1791

TUDOR, STANLY.

II Mary[2] Tudor (John[1]) married Capt. Thomas Stanly on (O. S.) 21 Jan. 1755 her first husband

Their child was

Thomas[3] b. 15 Jan. 1756 (O. S.) d. (drowned) 27 Nov. 1774. Her second husband, married 28 May 1760, was James Thompson. There was no issue by this marriage. He d. 15 May 1783

TUDOR, THOMPSON.

III Jane[2] Tudor (John[1]) married William Thompson on 14 May 1754. She died 28 Mar. 1791. He died 15 May 1787

Their children were four

1 John Tudor[3] b. 15 Oct. 1757 d. 1758 S. P.
2 William[3] b. 24 July 1760 d. 14 May 1780 S. P.
3 James[3] b. 6 Jan. 1767 d. 7 Dec 1783 S. P.
4 Henry[3] b. 20 Feb. 1771 d. 18 Jnne 1775 S. P.

TUDOR, SAVAGE.

V Elizabeth[2] Tudor (John[1]) married Habijah Savage on 9 May 1765. She died 1 Feb. 1788

Their children were eleven

1 John[3] b. 18 Apr. 1766 d. S. P.
2 Jane[3] b. 17 Feb. 1768
3 Elizabeth[3] b. 15 Apr. 1770
4 Deborah[3] b. 2 Mar. 1772 d. unmarried
5 Habijah[3] b. 24 Aug. 1775 d. 1 Oct. 1776
6 William[3] b. 28 Aug. 1777 d. 4 Nov. 1778
7 William[3] b. 30 Aug. 1779
8 Habijah[3] b. 5 July 1781 d. S. P.
9 James[3] b. 13 July 1784
10 Thomas[3] b. 11 Feb. 1786
11 Arthur[3] b. 1 Feb. 1787, married late in life, died S. P.

(7) William[3] Savage (John[1] Elizabeth[2]) married 1st Mary Ingersoll, married 2d Harriet Hooper of Newburyport. There were no children by 2d marriage. He died 30 June 1851

Their child by first marriage was

Mary Elizabeth[4] b. 1 Oct. 1807

Addenda, to line 4 below Tudor, Savage, add "at Boston 13 June 1838," to line 7 ditto, add "March 1831", to line 11 ditto, add "at St. Pierre, Martinique, 18 April 1803", to line 13 ditto, add "d. at New Orleans 18 July 1836".

(9) James 3 Savage (John 1 Elizabeth 2) married April 1823 Elizabeth Otis, widow of James Otis Lincoln. He died 8 March 1873

Their children were four

1 Emma 4 b. 4 March 1824, married 20 June, 1845 Prof. William Barton Rogers of the University of Virginia b. Dec. 1804 in Philadelphia, President and founder of the Mass. Inst. of Technology, who died S. P. 30 May 1882

2 Harriet 4 b. 10 Oct. 1826, d. 18 July 1854, married 6 Nov. 1851 Amos Binney of Boston

They had one child Lucy b. 30 Oct. 1852 d. 8 May 1854

3 Lucy 4 b. 11 Sep. 1829 d. 11 May 1850

4 James 4 b. 21 April 1832, Lieut. Col. 2d Mass. Vol. d. 22 Oct. 1862 of wounds at Charlottesville, Va., after battle of Cedar Mountain 9 Aug. 1862

(10) Thomas 3 (John 1 Elizabeth 2) married Lydia V. de Foucade

Their children were three

1 Thomas Francis 4 b. 1814 d. 1816

2 James Osgood 4 b. 15 Aug. 1819, M. D. 1839, d. 21 July 1861 at Havana, S. P.

3 Thomas 4 b. 27 Aug. 1823. He married first in 1850 Mary D. Lucena

Their children by first marriage were six

1 Thomas Emanuel 5 b. 17 April 1853

2 Nicholas 5 b. 26 May 1854 d. 26 May 1854

3 Josephine 5 b. 1855 d. 1855

4 Mary Mercedes 5 b. 8 Jan. 1857

5 Emma Blanche 5 b. 26 Aug. 1858

6 James 5 b. 1860 d. 1860 He married second, 20 Jan. 1870 at Panama Antonia Maldonado

The child by second marriage was

7 Arthur 5 b. 5 Dec. 1872 d. 26 March 1873

TUDOR.

(4) Frederic 3 Tudor (John 1 William 2) married at Mt. Upton, N. Y. 2 Jan. 1834, Euphemia Fenno, b. 6 Apr. 1814, daughter of Upton Fenno and Euphemia Johnston. He died 6 Feb. 1864 at Boston. She died 9 Mar. 1884 at Newbury, Vt.

Their children were six

1 Euphemia 4 b. 18 Feb. 1837
2 Frederic 4 b. 11 Feb. 1845
3 Delia Jarvis 4 b. 20 Mar. 1847
4 William 4 b. 27 Sep. 1848
5 Eleonora Elizabeth 4 b. 1 July 1850
6 Henry 4 b. 21 Jan. 1854

(8) Henry James 3 Tudor (John 1 William 2) married 5 Aug. 1844 Fanny Hortense Foster, b. 25 Dec. 1816, daughter of James Foster.

He died at Boston 27 Nov. 1864. She died at Paris, France, 1 Apr. 1892

Their children were three

1 Fanny 4 b. 18 Feb. 1846 d. 18 Dec. 1855 at Boston
2 Emma 4 b. 1848 d. 28 May 1850 at Boston
3 Virginia 4 b. 27 May 1850 d. 19 July 1886 at Paris, France

(2) Frederic 4 Tudor (John 1 William 2 Frederic 3) married in Boston 24 June 1867, Louisa Simes, b. 20 Sep. 1845, adopted daughter of Joseph Simes of Plymouth

Their children are five

1 Frederic 5 b. 26 Mar. 1869
2 Marie Louise 5 b. 23 July 1870
3 Emma Cecile 5 b. 25 Mar. 1871
4 Euphemia 5 b. 7 Sep. 1875
5 Rosamond 5 b. 20 June 1878

(4) William[4] Tudor (John[1] William[2] Frederic[3]) married at Paris, France, 24 May, 1873, Elizabeth Whitwell, b. 29 April 1851, daughter of William Scollay Whitwell and Mary Hubbard

Their children are five.

1 Henry Dubois[5] b. 30 Oct, 1874 at Paris, France
2 William[5] b. 14 Jan. 1876 at Boston
3 Elizabeth[5] b. 27 Nov. 1878 at Boston
4 Delia Aimee[5] b. 22 Apr. 1880 at Marietta, Georgia
5 Mary[5] b. 30 July 1886 at Paris, France

TUDOR, KLECZKOWSKI.

(1) Euphemia[4] Tudor (John[1] William[2] Frederic[3]) married at Singapore, India, 12 April 1872 Michel Alexandre Cholewa, Count Kleczkowski, b. 28 Feb. 1818, only son of Count Joseph Kleczkowski and Julie Sobieska, a direct descendant of John Sobieski, King of Poland. He died 26 Mar. 1886

Their children are four

1 Euphemia Alice Alexandrine Marie[5] b. 18 Apr. 1863 at Pekin, China, married at Paris, France, Barnard Hutchinson, son of Alcander Hutchinson, formerly of Boston
2 Eleonora Delia Julie Aimee[5] b. 3 Jan. 1866 at Paris, France
3 Frederic Tudor Alexandre Paul Henry[5] b. 17 Oct 1871 at Versailles, France
4 Yvonne Jeanne Michelene Isabelle Virginie[5] b. 25 Feb. 1880 at Paris, France

XXVII

TUDOR, WILMER.

(3) Delia Jarvis[4] Tudor (John[1] William[2] Frederic[3]) married in Boston 15 June 1871 Skipwith Wilmer b. 21 Feb. 1843 a son of Bishop Joseph Wilmer and Helen Skipwith of Virginia she died 15 Oct. 1879

Their children were four

1 Ephemia Fenno[5] b. 28 April 1872 d. 5 May 1873
2 Joseph Pere Bell[5] b. 5 Sep. 1873 d. 1 June 1874
3 Helen Skipwith[5] b. 2 Aug. 1876
4 Delia Tudor[5] b. 10 Oct. 1879

TUDOR, HART.

(5) Eleonora Elizabeth[4] Tudor (John[1] William[2] Frederic[3]) married in Boston 4 Oct. 1871 Frederick Lestrange Hart of Montreal Canada b. 27 Jan. 1851

Their children are four

1 Mary Edith Effie Tudor[5] b. 19 Sep. 1872
2 Ernest Percyval Tudor[5] b. 27 Dec. 1873
3 Edith Ethel Alice[5] b. 8 Mar. 1876
4 William Owen Tudor[5] b. 20 Feb. 1884

TUDOR, GARLAND.

(2) Marie Louise[5] Tudor (John,[1] William,[2] Frederic,[3] Frederic[4]) married 20 Sep. 1893 at Boston James Albert Garland of New York b. 26 Nov. 1870

Their children are two

James Albert[6] b. 10 May 1894
Tudor[6] b. 9 July 1895

TUDOR, CONVERSE.

(3) Emma Cecile[5] Tudor (John,[1] William,[2] Frederic,[3] Frederic[4]) married at Boston 6 June 1894 Frederick Shepherd Converse of Newton b. 5 Jan. 1871

They have one child

Emma Louise[6] b. 1 April 1895

TUDOR, GARDINER.

(5) Emma Jane[3] Tudor (John[1] William[2]) married in 1805 Robert Hallowell Gardiner. He was b. 1782 d. 1864. She died 1865

Their children were nine

1 Emma Jane[4] b. 1806 d. 1845 S. P.

2 Anne Hallowell[4] b. 1807

3 Robert Hallowell[4] { b. 1809 m. 1842 Sarah Fenwick Jones b. 1814 d. 1869 He d. 1886 S. P. }

4 Delia Tudor[4] { b. 1812 m. 1834 George Jones d. S. P. 1836 }

5 Lucy Vaughan[4] b. 1814 d. 1847 S. P.

6 John William Tudor[4] b. 1817

7 Henrietta[4] b. 1820 m. 1846 Richard Sullivan She d. S. P. 1880

8 Frederic[4] b. 11 Sep. 1822 at Oaklands Maine

9 Eleanor Harriet[4] b. 16 July 1825 at Oaklands Maine

(6) Colonel John William Tudor[4] Gardiner (John[1] William[2] Emma Jane[3]) Married in 1854 Anne Elizabeth (Hays) West b. 1821 he died 1879

Their children were six

1 Robert Hallowell[5] b. 1855

2 Eleanor[5] b. 1857

3 Ann Hays[5] b. 1859 d. 1860
4 Francis Richards[5] b. 1860 d. 1880
5 John Hays[5] } twins b. 1863
6 John Tudor[5] }

TUDOR, GARDINER, RICHARDS

(2) Anne Hallowell[4] Gardiner (John,[1] William,[2] Emma Jane[3]) married 1832 at Gardiner Me. Francis Richards b. 1805. She died 1858. He died 1858

Their children were seven

1 Francis Gardiner[5] b. 10 June 1833
2 George Henry[5] b. 1837 d. 1837
3 George Henry[5] b. 14 June 1838
4 Sarah[5] b. 2 Jan. 1840 d. 2d Sept. 1855
5 John Tudor[5] b. 23 July 1841
6 Robert Hallowell[5] b. 26 Aug 1844 married 4 June 1875 Ellen H. Swallow
7 Henry[5] b. 17 July 1848

(1) Francis Gardiner[5] Richards (John[1] William[2] Emma Jane[3]) married in 1807 Annie Ashburner, daughter of Samuel Ashburner of London Eng. He died 10 Feb. 1884

Their children are two

1 Francis Ashburner[6] b. 22 Feb. 1880
2 Anne Hallowell[6] b. Aug. 1881

(5) John Tudor[5] Richards (John,[1] William,[2] Emma Jane[3]) married in Paris France 18 June 1870 Cora Howard, daughter of Benjamin Chandler Howard

Their children are four

1 Amy[6] b. 15 July 1871
2 Madeleine[6] b. 26 Oct 1873
3 Dorothy[6] b. 15 Mar. 1877 d. 30 Oct. 1878
4 Ruth[6] b. 4 May 1881

(7) Henry[5] Richards (John[1] William[2] Emma Jane[3]) married 17 June 1871 Laura Elizabeth Howe, daughter of Dr. Samuel S. Howe and Julia Ward.
Their children are seven
1 Alice Maud[6] b. 24 June 1872
2 Rosalind[6] b. 30 June 1874
3 Henry Howe[6] b. 23 Feb. 1876
4 Julia Ward[6] b. 30 Aug. 1878
5 Maud[6] b. 7 Nov. 1881 d. 11 Oct. 1882
6 John[6] b. 13 Feb 1884
7 Laura Elizabeth[6] b. 12 Feb. 1886

(8) Rev Frederic[4] Gardiner (John,[1] William,[2] Emma Jane[3]) married 25 Aug 1846 Caroline Vaughan daughter of William Vaughan of Hallowell Me. he died 17 July 1889
Their children were five
1 Emma Jane[5] b. 16 Oct 1847 at Saco Me
2 William Tudor[5] b. 8 Apr. 1856 at Lewiston Me d. 21 Dec 1862 at Gardiner Me.
3 Frederic[5] b. 5 Apr. 1858 at Oaklands Me.
4 Henrietta[5] b. 26 Feb 1860 at Oaklands Me
5 Alfred[5] b. 12 Apr 1862 at Gardiner d. 1 Aug 1877, drowned at Swan Island Me.

(1) Robert Hallowell[5] Gardiner (John,[1] William,[2] Emma Jane[3]) married Alice Bangs, daughter of Edward Bangs of Boston

Their children are five

1 Robert Hallowell[6] b. 5 Nov. 1882
2 Alice[6] b. 24 Feb. 1885
3 Silvester[6] b. 11 Jan. 1888 d. 15 May 1889
4 Anna Lowell[6] b. 9 Sep. 1890
5 William Tudor[6] b. 12 June 1892

(3) Rev. Frederic[5] Gardiner (John,[1] William,[2] Emma Jane[3]) married 1885 Sallie Merrick daughter of William H. Merrick of Germantown Penn.

Their children are three

1 Frederic Merrick[6] b. 27 June 1887 at Sioux Falls S. D.
2 William Henry[6] b. 5 May 1890 at Philadelphia
3 Frances Vaughan[6] b. 16 Sep. 1892 at Pomfret Conn.

TUDOR, GARDINER, FERGUSON.

(1) Emma Jane[5] Gardiner (John,[1] William,[2] Emma Jane[3]) married on 15 Oct 1873 Rev Henry Ferguson of Stamford Conn.

Their children are four

1 Samuel[6] b. 19 Nov. 1874
2 Eleanor Margaret[6] b. 30 June 1876
3 Henry Gardiner[6] b. 21 June 1882
4 Charles Vaughan[6] b. 15 Aug. 1885

TUDOR, SAVAGE, COOPER

(3) Elizabeth[3] Savage (John[1] Elizabeth[2]) married at Boston 23 June 1791. John Cooper b. 13 Dec. 1765 at Boston Son of William Cooper and Katharine Wendell. She died at Machias Me. 13 July 1854, he died at Cooper Me. 18 Nov. 1845

Their children were nine

1 John Tudor[4] b. 6 June 1792 d. S. P. 22 March 1812 at Cambridge
2 William[4] b. 3 Jan. 1794
3 Emma Elizabeth[4] b. 20 July 1796
4 Charles Wendell[4] b. 17 May 1798 d. S. P. 2 June 1825 at Havana Cuba
5 Samuel[4] b. 2 June 1800 d. 6 Apr. 1804 Machias Me.
6 James Sullivan[4] b. 10 Oct. 1802
7 Thomas Savage[4] b. 6 July 1805 d. 21 July 1805 at Machias
8 Caroline Savage[4] b. 28 April 1808
9 Arthur Savage[4] b. 9 May 1811 d. 21 Feb. 1818 at Machias

(2) William[4] Cooper (John[1] Elizabeth[2]) married 8 Aug. 1826 Eliza Balch Dutton of Lubec Me. b. 15 Dec. 1803. He died 27 Aug. 1875 at Dennyville Me. She died 16 Jan. 1844

Their children were nine
1 William Savage[5] b. 25 July 1827
2 Elizabeth Dutton[5] b. 19 Nov. 1828
3 Emma Porter[5] b. 27 Aug. 1830
4 Caroline Pearson[5] b. 11 Jan. 1832 d. S. P. 16 Dec. 1877 at Dennysville Me.
5 Helen Marston[5] b. 26 July 1834
6 Harriet Coolidge[5] b. 8 June 1836 d. S. P. 9 May 1841 at Cooper Me.
7 John[5] b. 22 Nov. 1838 d. 24 Nov. 1838 at Cooper
8 Mary[5] b. 7 Sep. 1839
9 Harriet Cooledge b. 4 Sep. 1841

(6) James Sullivan[4] Cooper (John[1] Elizabeth[2]) married first at Boston 28 May 1832 Mary Elizabeth Sav-

Errata in line 7 for "1804 Machias" read "1804 at Machias", in line 16 for "Dennyville" read "Dennysville" and in line 17 for "16 Jan. 1844" read "13 July 1854".

age[4] daughter of William Savage[3] of Boston. She died 7 Apr. 1842

Their children were three

1 Mary Ingersoll[5] b. 3 March 1833 unmarried.

2 William Savage[5] b. 26 Dec. 1837 d. 26 Sep 1839 at Calais Me

3 Harriet Savage[5] b. 16 Sep. 1841 d. 16 Sep 1842 at Calais Me. He married second at Haverhill Mass 1 Oct. 1845 Abigail Ingersoll Girdler b. 10 May 1817 daughter of Capt. John Girdler and Abigail Ingersoll He died 28 July 1870 at Amherst Mass

Their children were four

4 Elizabeth Savage[5] b. 21 Sep. 1846

5 James Ingersoll[5] b. 7 Apr. 1849

6 Charles Wendell[5] b. 16 May 1851

7 Alice Girdler[5] b. 15 June 1857

(1) William Savage[5] Cooper (John[1] Elizabeth[2]) married at Sonora Cal. 17 May 1864 Sarah Jane Darling.

They have one child

1 Jennie May b. 6 May 1865 at Sonora Cal.

(6) Charles Wendell[5] Cooper M.D. (John[1] Elizabeth[2]) married at New York 8 Sep. 1861 Elizabeth Savage[6] Porter, daughter of John Cooper[5] Porter, of St. Louis

Their children are two

1 Anna Porter[6] b. 30 Oct. 1885 at Northampton Mass.

2 Ruth[6] b. 31 Mar. 1891 at Northampton Mass.

TUDOR, SAVAGE, COOPER.

(3) Emma Elizabeth[4] Cooper (John,[1] Elizabeth[2]) married at Machias 20 Oct. 1820 Rufus King Porter She died 26 Oct 1827 at Portland Me.

Their children were four

1 Emma Jane[5] b. 4 Sept 1821 d. 19 July 1866. S. P.
2 Charles Wendell[5] b. 1 May 1823
3 John Cooper[5] b. 6 Feb. 1825
4 Caroline Elizabeth[5] b. 20 Nov. 1826

(8) Caroline Savage[4] Cooper (John[1] Elizabeth[2]) married at Cooper Me 28 Nov. 1836 Rev. William John Newman of Andover Mass She died 3 Sep. 1871 at Andover

They had one child

1 Emma Elizabeth[5] b. 8 Mar 1838 at Stratham N. H.

(2) Elizabeth Dutton[5] Cooper (John[1] Elizabeth[2]) married first 29 Oct 1853 Hon Luther Stearns Cushing there was no issue to this marriage & she on 17 Nov. 1858 married second Rev Edward Henry Buck She died 24 June 1862

They had one child

1 Amelia Duryée[6] b. 3 Dec. 1859

(5) Helen Marston[5] Cooper (John[1] Elizabeth[2]) married 8 Feb 1864, George E. Bugbee

Their children are three all born at Oakland Cal.

1 George Louis[6] b. June 1869
2 Alice Cooper[6] b. 1 Sep. 1871
3 Frederick William[6] b. 1 Dec. 1875

(8) Mary[5] Cooper (John[1] Elizabeth[2]) married 12 Jan. 1864, Frederick J. Gardner

Their children are two

1 Maria Lincoln[6] b. 9 Mar 1868 at Dennysville, Me.
2 Harriet Cooper[6] b. 31 Aug 1870 at Dennysville, Me.

(9) Harriet Coolidge[5] Cooper (John[1] Elizabeth[2]) married 24 Oct 1867 Edward B. Kelly

They had one child

1 Frank Edward[6] b. 16 July 1868 d. 10 Aug 1868

(4) Elizabeth Savage[5] Cooper (John[1] Elizabeth[2]) married 13 Oct 1875 at Amherst Mass, Dr. John Gilbert Stanton

They have one child

1 Alice Cooper[6] b. 27 July 1879 at New London

(7) Alice Girdler[5] Cooper (John[1] Elizabeth[2]) married 6 Sep. 1881 at Amherst, Frederick Tuckerman of Amherst Mass

Their children are two

1 Margaret b. 6 June 1884
2 Frederika b. 23 April 1888

TUDOR, SAVAGE, COOPER, PORTER

(2) Charles Wendell[5] Porter (John[1] Elizabeth[2]) married at Batavia Ill. 1 Sep 1864 Susan Ellen Lockwood daughter of Hon. Samuel D. Lockwood Associate Justice of the Supreme Court of Ill.

Their children are three

1 Mary King[6] b.
2 Harriet Eager[6] b.
3 Anna Lockwood[6] b.

(3) John Cooper[5] Porter (John[1] Elizabeth[2]) married at St. Louis, 9 June 1852, Anna McKee. She died 23 Nov. 1867

Their children were two

1 Elizabeth Savage[6] b. 9 April 1853 at St Louis
2 Charles Wendell[6] b. 9 Mar. 1866 at St Louis

Errata in line 8th from bottom, for "Eager b." read "Eddy b. 27 Oct. 1867".

Addenda, to line 10th from bottom add "born at Batavia, Ill." To line 9th ditto, add "8 June 1865", to line 7th ditto add "15 June 1869".

(1) Amelia Duryée[6] Buck (John,[1] Elizabeth[2]) married at Philadelphia 26 Sep. 1893, Lyman Johnson
They have one child
1 Barbara[7] b. 11 Nov. 1894 at Sioux Rapids Iowa

TUDOR, SAVAGE, BRUCE.

Jane[3] Savage (John[1] Elizabeth[2]) married Phineas Bruce lawyer b. 7 Jan. (or June) 1762 son of George Bruce & Hannah Lovett of Mendon Mass. at Machias, March 1795 she died at Cambridge Mass 1845 he died in Uxbridge Mass. 9 Oct. 1809
Their children were six, all born at Machias
1 George W.[4] b. 7 Jan. 1796
2 Henry[4] b. 12 Feby. 1798
3 Edward[4] b. 3 July 1799
4 Mary[4] b. 7 June 1801 d. 25 Nov. 1801
5 James Savage[4] b. 25 Nov. 1802
6 William Savage[4] b. 28 Nov. 1804

Commodore Henry[4] Bruce U. S. Navy (John[1] Elizabeth[2]) married Miss Marston b. he died she died
Their children were six
1 Jane[5] b. d. unmarried
2 Eliza[5] b. married Mr. Ryan and left one child
3 (James)[5]?
4
5 Mary[5] b. d. unmarried
6 Sarah[5] b. married Philip Voorhees, son of Admiral Philip K. Voorhees

James Savage[4] Bruce (John[1] Elizabeth[2]) married
Their children were two
1 James[5] b. d. young
2 Emma[5] b. d. unmarried

Delia Tudor Stewart

XXXVII

TUDOR, STEWART

(6) Delia[3] Tudor (John[1] William[2]) married Charles Stewart Commodore U. S. Navy on 25 Nov 1813 b. she died 7 Sept 1861 at Dublin Ire. he died

Their children were three

1 Charles Tudor[4] b. d. S. P. Rome 8 apr 1874

2 Delia Tudor[4] b. 1814

3

TUDOR, STEWART, PARNELL.

(2) Delia Tudor[4] Stewart (John,[1] William,[2] Delia[3]) married May 1834 John Henry Parnell of Avondale Ireland b. 1811 d. 1859

Their children are ten

1 Delia Stewart[5] b. 1837 m. James Thomson d. 188

2 Hayes[5] b. d. 1853 Nice France

3 Emily[5] b. m. 1865 Capt Dickinson

4 Sophia[5] b. m. Alfred MacDermott Barrister of Dublin. She died but left children

5 John Howard[5] b.

6 Charles Stewart[5] b. 28 June 1846 m. Kate O'Shea 25 June 1891 d. S. P. at Brighton Eng. 6 Oct. 1891

7 Fanny[5] b. 1848 d. 1882 at Boston Mass. S. P.

8 Annie Mercer[5] b.

9 Henry Tudor[5] b. 1850

10 Theodosia[5] b. m. Lieut. Claude Paget

INDEX OF NAMES IN DIARY.

INDEX TO GENEALOGY AND PAGES WITH ROMAN NUMERALS.

www.ingramcontent.com/pod-product-compliance
Lightning Source LLC
Chambersburg PA
CBHW020008030726
47500CB00002B/492
* 9 7 8 3 3 3 7 0 0 7 4 1 6 *